All

This

Happened

in the

Tenth Century…

~

Sequel to the book
Captured by Vikings
by Torill Thorstad Hauger

Escape from the Vikings

Written and Illustrated by
Torill Thorstad Hauger

Translated from the Norwegian by
Anne Born

Edited by
Lisa Hamnes

ESCAPE FROM THE VIKINGS

Published 2000 by
SKANDISK, INC.
6667 West Old Shakopee Road, Suite 109
Bloomington, Minnesota 55438

ISBN 1-57534-013-5

English edition Copyright © 2000 Skandisk, Inc.
Illustrations Copyright © 2000 Torill Thorstad Hauger
Translated from the original Norwegian edition, published 1979
by Gyldendal Norsk Forlag, Oslo, Norway, under the title *Flukten fra vikingene*
Copyright in all countries signatory to the Berne and Universal Conventions

Written and illustrated by Torill Thorstad Hauger
Translated by Anne Born
Edited by Lisa Hamnes

Library of Congress Cataloging-in-Publication Data

Hauger, Torill Thorstad, 1943-
 [Flukten fra vikingene. English]
 Escape from the Vikings / Torill Thorstad Hauger ; translated by Anne Born.
    p. cm.
Summary: After being taken to Norway as slaves, an Irish brother and sister sail with
their Norwegian master to Iceland, where they spend an adventurous year, all the time
dreaming of returning home to Ireland.
 ISBN 1-57534-013-5
 1. Iceland--History--To 1262--Juvenile fiction. [1. Iceland--History--To 1262--Fiction. 2.
Vikings--Fiction. 3. Slaves--Fiction. 4. Brothers and sisters--Fiction. 5. Ireland--History
--To 1172--Fiction.] I. Born, Anne. II. Title.
 PZ7.H28665 Es 2000
 [Fic]--dc21
                                              00-041322

Manufactured in the United States of America

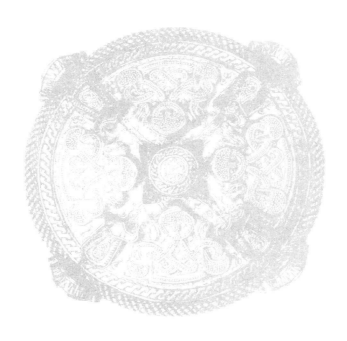

Chapter One

*T*ir pulled the sheepskin more closely around her. She was cold and shivering. It was cramped in the little cave and she tried to make herself invisible. Her heart beat hard and painfully in her chest. Wouldn't they come soon? she thought. Wouldn't Reim come soon? Her arms and legs were stiff from sitting waiting like this. Behind the hill the moon began to climb up the sky. It stared at her with a cold pale face before it was hidden by the flying clouds again. Did it bode good or ill tonight, she wondered?

It was the second time she had sat and waited tensely like this. The first time had been in a low, icy-cold slaves' house in the Vikings' homeland, Norway. Then they had managed to get away and cross the great sea to Iceland. Now they were about to set out on an even longer and more perilous journey. Down on the beach, not more than a hundred paces from her hiding-place, three ships lay ready to sail. They would set a southerly course past the islands in the Atlantic Ocean and straight for Ireland.

So much had happened since that summer when they had been seized by the Vikings and taken away from their homeland. When she closed her eyes she could still see the red tongues of flame licking up over the monastery church in her village. She could hear the screams of fleeing grown ups and children, she could see the menacing dragon-like ships anchored in the fjord. Now it seemed an eternity since she had heard her mother tongue, an eternity since anyone had called them Patrick and Sunniva, which had been their *names when she and her brother ran around in the green fields at home in Ireland.*

Down on the beach the men had almost finished carrying barrels and sacks on board. A single guard kept watch on one ship. He leaned against the mast singing a sad monotonous song that made her drowsy.

Tir rested her head on her arms, and behind her closed eyes pictures arose from their first days in the strange land far in the north.

That autumn day when they set sail from Norway clouds swept across the sky and the sea was gray with foaming white crests. Aud's great dragon ship was first out of the fjord; three more ships followed with all sails set.

"What do you think it will be like in the new country?" asked Tir. "Do you think it's true what people say, that both fire and water spout out of the ground, and the great pans boil and bubble where the troll hags cook up their brew?"

"I think so," Reim nodded. "I think it's true. Nowhere else on the great surface of the earth is there so much witchcraft and magic as in Iceland. Everyone says so."

"Brede too?"

"Yes, Brede too."

They talked a lot about that while they were on board ship. Suspense crawled just under their skin. They were on their way to a new unknown land far to the west over the sea. Behind them lay Norway, land of the Vikings. For a whole year they had toiled and slaved for a powerful earl before they managed to escape and make their way to Brede the farmer and his wife. Their new master and mistress were ordinary farmers who did not treat slaves very differently from people of their own kin. Now they had left poor soil and a strife-torn land in Norway to voyage to Iceland and build a new farmstead there. Also on board was Asbjørn, Brede's neighbor. He had sailed to Iceland before and knew the waters like the back of his hand. Asbjørn had brought his cattle and slaves and his whole family with him. Brede and Bergliot had their slaves and their three sons. The youngest boy, Ravn, was a real mad-cap who liked to show he was a man. He balanced on the ship's rail while the waves washed over the decks, and he climbed high up the mast. Bergliot had her work cut out keeping him under control.

Tir was not a very good sailor, but she did not once complain during the long voyage. "I have to pinch my arm to find out if it's really true," she said. "That we've really gotten away from the cold slaves' house, that I am finished with the heavy work of churning, that we don't need to be afraid any more of the earl's brutal men using their sticks on a poor slave's back. Everything will be better now—in the new country."

But Reim turned away.

"You mustn't forget we are still slaves," he said shortly. "And it's a long way from Iceland to our homeland."

～

As time went on many people began to regret setting out on such a long and dangerous voyage so late in the year. In the middle of the ocean the northwesterly came roaring at them. Thunder rolled across the sky and the rain whipped the sea white. The ships were parted from each other and danced like little nutshells on the raging sea. The low homespun tent erected before the mast did not offer much shelter. It was crammed with all manner of things: leather sacks and chests, bundles of clothing

10 and big iron pots. In a sort of pen sunk into the deck the poor domestic animals stood bleating and mooing, fearful of the rough sea. They sailed on for days and nights with no slackening of the wind. Not until after more than thirty days at sea did anything happen.

Asbjørn stood battling with the tiller, frost in his hair and beard. He spat to get the taste of salt out of his mouth: "We've been tossing around in this miserable gale for an eternity without seeing so much as a rock sticking up out of the sea. I'm afraid it's like the troll at Utgard!"

"It doesn't look encouraging," Brede replied. His words were almost lost in the wind. "We're nearly out of food and fresh water."

Then it was Tir who caught sight of the bird circling high in the air. She saw it clearly through the opening in the tarpaulin. The bird was such a strange color. In the dull morning light its wings had an almost blue sheen. She wondered whether to shake Reim. He was breathing heavily, half-asleep with his face buried deep in a sheepskin. But she went on watching the bird wonderingly. It reminded her of something. Of a story she had heard back home in Ireland. Something about a bird flying on strong wings over the great wide ocean...

Then she heard a shout:

"Land ho!"

Tir got to her feet. She pulled the sheepskin over her head and crawled out of the shelter. Ugh, what a gale was blowing out there! The waves struck the ship's side and sent spray high in the air. She glanced up at the mast. There were several birds circling up there. They rose and sank in the air.

"Land ahead," came shouts all over the ship. "Land ahead!"

Children and grown ups crawled towards the bow,

where the breakers broke into whipping rain over the deck planking. Far away on the horizon, where sea and sky merged, they could see a narrow strip of land. It came in sight each time the ship rose to plough through a new crest.

"By Odin, what's all this uproar?"

A voice of thunder broke through the sound of wind and waves. Out of the tent lurched a gigantic figure. He looked more like a grizzly bear than a human being. His hair was tousled, and he flailed his huge fists around him.

"What's all this uproar, I say. I only just crawled under my sheepskin and you have to roar as if the sea god himself was after you!" He scowled at the people around him with red-rimmed eyes. "Una!" he roared. "Where is Una?"

A heavyset young woman hurried towards the tent. She battled against the wind and barely managed to keep on her feet on the rocking deck. Her hair blew about beneath her kerchief, like a bright mane around her head. When she reached the giant she seized hold of his homespun jacket to steady herself.

"Digralde," she said. "Over there is the land we have been longing for." She pointed to the northwest. "Our little daughter is waiting for us there! If all goes well we shall build our farmstead there!"

She nodded and smiled at a lad standing close by. It was her brother, Vidur.

Digralde rubbed his eyes and stared. Then he opened his mouth and let out a rousing yell. It boomed over the sea as if the god of thunder himself was on board.

"By the cats of Freya," he roared. "Haven't you got eyes in your heads, my good people! Can't you see we're nearing Iceland!"

He seized the small woman round her waist and lifted her up. "Now life begins, Una! This very moment!"

"Let go of me," scolded Una, dangling between deck and sky. "Let go of me, or you'll put an end to my life, anyway!"

At that moment a breaker knocked them over and left them floundering about at the bottom of the boat. The women pulled the children with them and crept under the tarpaulin again. Brede grabbed his son's ear: "You ought to know better, Ravn, than to lean out over the rail in this gale! Fetch the bailer, boy. Everyone must take

turns now."

The men battled their way forward. The ship's prow bore a carved dragon. It looked threatening with its gaping jaw and vacant empty eye sockets.

"Ahoy, there, heave ho now!" They dragged and pulled at the dragonhead. Suddenly a new breaker came pouring over the rail and almost knocked them over. The dragon was not easy to deal with. It seemed to stiffen its neck and resist with all its strength. Brede said afterwards that it seemed to utter a deep growl when they finally managed to get the head down into the bottom of the ship.

"It's best like that," said Mistress Bergliot. "We can't be too careful. They must be standing there on shore now. They stand on the gray mountains watching us sail in. The land spirits have lived in stones and mountains in Iceland for thousands of years. Now they fear we will take their land away from them. We mustn't terrify them with gaping animal jaws."

~

They had come so close to land that the cliffs reared up like a wall against them. The smallest slave girl crept close to Tir, and held on tight round her waist. "I'm frightened," she whimpered. "The whole world is rocking up and down."

Tir shut her eyes every time the bow dipped down into a new foaming surging wave. Each moment she expected the ship to be splintered on underwater reefs that must be lurking in these waters.

A big breaker swept in over the stern. Brede swore loudly. One of the barrels of corn vanished with the rush of water and sailed away over the rail. Brede threw himself at it but had to grip firmly so as not to be sucked down into the depths. Drenched to the skin and with blood seeping from a wound on his forehead, he crawled up again. "Reef the sails," he yelled. "We're nearing land!"

They got out the oars in frantic haste.

Asbjørn stood at the tiller. He set course for a narrow bay where the waters rushed inward with bubbling foam. When the sea retreated snarling, the shore was almost dry, with rocks standing up like sharp spines. Asbjørn pushed the tiller over and steered into the bay.

Then it happened. The ship was thrown into the maelstrom. A violent thud shook the whole ship. The poles holding the tent broke. Sote the horse neighed loudly and struck out with his forefeet, and Digralde had to use all his strength to hold back the animal. Half blinded by the spray and deafened by the noise of the waves, the men staggered about. "There is a gash in the hull," shouted Asbjørn. "The ship is taking in water!"

Tir and Reim clutched each other in terror. "St. Patrick and all the saints aid us!" Soon they would sink down into the icy cold dark water off the coast of a new and unknown land. The little slave girl screamed and screamed while sea and waves were one huge boiling mass, and the wind howled around them.

Then something happened that later seemed like a miracle. Suddenly they were hurled away from off the underwater reef and drawn on a great wave into the bay. When the ship grounded on the sand the men jumped out and began to pull the ship with all their might. They hauled and pulled every time a new wave came rushing under the keel. When the ship was finally safe they started to get the animals ashore. It was a terrible frantic toiling. They battled in icy water up to their waists, and dragged and carried the heavy animal bodies. Only then did they see that four of the sheep had died, and several leather sacks and chests had disappeared in the foaming waters.

"Freya be praised we've made it at last," whispered Asbjørn's wife to him. She clasped the little slave girl to her. The child went on weeping. She had hurt herself badly when the ship rolled over, and lost some baby teeth in her fall. She sobbed and shivered in her soaking clothes.

Tir pushed some wet locks of hair from her forehead.

She could not see much of the land through the driving snow. Bare mountains loomed up everywhere, and west of the bay a foaming river rushed out into the sea. Iceland...the name suited this country well. It was cold and inhospitable. It was like a mythical country where no human beings lived.

Asbjørn pointed up the mountainside at a little building just visible through the falling snow. It must be an isolated hay barn or a summer pasture cottage.

All around the landscape was deserted as far as the eye could see. The snow drifted and covered the ground with a blanket of slushy gray-white that concealed all tracks and traces of people.

The little group started to move up the hillside. Some sacks of corn and clothes chests were loaded on to Sote. They had to carry the rest on their backs. Tir and Reim brought up the rear driving the flock of sheep and goats before them.

There had been scant room on board the ship, but there was still less in the small shack that was more like a little hovel built of stone and turf. The children found a corner each for themselves, and snuggled close to the animals to keep warm. Wet jackets and outer garments hung dripping from the beams.

Digralde stood up and fastened his belt. "There is nothing left but a dried leg of mutton," he said, "and that is lean fare for Digralde." He threw a hide over his shoulders and rummaged for some tools in a sack under the beams. Then he went out into the storm with Vidur and Asbjørn. Before the close of evening they came tramping into the hut, their clothes and bodies frozen stiff but carrying a big wooden crate. It was full of shining silver fish. "Anyone who has been to Iceland before knows you only have to scoop them out of the sea," said Asbjørn. "There's enough food here for a whole king's household and more. But ugh, how it blows out on the reefs!"

After days of heavy snowfall the weather eased. Brede took his sons with him and went down to the beach to look at the ship. There was a big gash in the hull that would take some time to mend.

Every day they went fishing or hunted birds, which seemed to be plentiful here. One evening, the men came back late from hunting. They had caught two small seals which they threw down outside in the snow. Now they had enough food for a long time.

But when they came inside their faces were grave. They hung up their capes and leather cloaks without a word, and took their seats on the bench in silence.

"This is a strange company we have with us," said Bergliot. "I really believe you have all lost your tongues!"

"It is not always so easy to loosen tongues," said Brede in a low voice. "Three other ships set sail from Norway with us. Now we know what happened to one of those ships."

Silence fell over the room. Even the smallest children who had been crawling around on the floor playing sat down to listen to what Brede had to tell.

"We were hunting out on the furthest reefs," said Brede, "at roughly the place where our ship was nearly crushed to matchwood when we reached Iceland. We had just shot the second seal when Vidur called out that he could see something floating along in the sea. I felt shocked straight away. It was a brown jacket bobbing about on the water. When we came near the cliff we saw the beach below was covered with shattered chests that had floated ashore.

Then we caught sight of the ship. It was lying bow upward just off the cliff. It seemed as if the god of the sea himself had stretched out a gigantic hand and pulled the hull down into the depths. Everyone on board now lies at rest deep down in Njord's kingdom."

"That is how it went with many of our kinsmen, then," said Bergliot softly. She let her hands fall on her lap. From the beach came the roar of the breakers like distant thunder.

~

"I can see a man riding over there in the pass!" Ravn kept on shouting, and ran to and fro in front of the house.

The man turned and rode towards them. He was wrapped in a gray homespun cloak the same color as the horse's coat. It was as if man and horse had grown together.

He shook his head in wonderment when he heard about their voyage. Not many people dared the sea at this time of year. But he knew who they were at once, for word had gone around that Aud had made safe landing. Now she had acquired land in Iceland, and the slaves had already begun to build the house.

"Is it far from here?" asked Brede.

"No further than if you sail east when day breaks, you will be there before the sun is high in the sky."

Asbjørn mentioned the names of his kin. The Icelander nodded. He recognized several of the names. If Asbjørn wished, he could hire him some horses so that he could build where his kinsmen had settled.

Some time later the Icelander returned with six small, long-haired horses. Asbjørn and his people began to load the horses and pack up their belongings. Then they set off. The little slave girl was allowed to ride with the master himself. She rode backward and waved to Tir and Reim as long as she could see them and they her.

A few days later the ship was ready to sail. Brede and Bergliot worked hard to get all their things on board. Then the ship set course westward with a fresh favorable wind. The sun shone from an icy cold, pale green winter sky. Tir stood by the rail looking at the land. One mountain after another rose out of the morning mist. She saw foaming rivers rushing out into the sea, blue hills and woods with trees white with frost; and above it all, shining glaciers arching over the mountains, with sharp spines and peaks of ice.

Iceland was a beautiful country, after all.

~

Aud was out in the yard when the ship sailed in. She asked the slaves to go down to the beach and help carry the baggage ashore. Then she went down to talk with Brede. She took both of his hands.

"You are welcome, Brede, my kinsman. The gods be praised that you and your people came safely across the sea. That has not happened to all those who sailed from Norway..."

"No, that's true," said Brede quietly. He stood gazing thoughtfully ahead of him. They had arrived at an extensive settlement, surrounded by low mountains. A broad, deep river flowed through the middle of the valley. The farms were spread out, with large pastures between them. Flocks of goats and sheep were digging for fodder under the snow, and everywhere were the small long-haired horses that were so plentiful in this land.

Aud had brought big spruce tree trunks with her, hewn before she left Norway. They only needed to put up the trunks when they arrived safely in Iceland. The slaves built the house quickly. Now her farmhouse stood in the settlement, its new timbers shining.

Brede bent his head to get through the door. He sat down on the bench. Aud bade her kinsman drink a welcome toast.

"Now you can see what my new hall is like. The smoke from the hearth hasn't covered the walls with soot as yet. It seems strange to think of the farmhouse I left at home in Norway. It was black with age, and six generations had passed their lives under its low roof. But I wanted to try something new for myself and my sons."

Brede laughed. "Yes, no one can accuse you of lacking courage."

Aud put her hand on her kinsman's shoulder. "I advise you to take some land a little further north in the valley, Brede. There are good pastures there that no one has claimed yet."

Brede nodded. "So it's getting crowded in this country as well. I have to think of my sons. The eldest are getting to the age when it wouldn't surprise me if they each found a wife here in Iceland, and set up their own farmsteads."

Aud's eyes sparkled. "What about your youngest son, then? "Ravn is a bright enough boy," laughed Brede, "but he's a bit too much of a wild one for a poor father to cope with." "Oh, well," smiled Aud. "Maybe you don't remember what you were like yourself at that age. You were more often up in the treetops than down in the field."

Aud raised her drinking horn to toast her kinsman, but at that moment they heard shouts and merry laughter out in the farmyard. Aud turned to the small window to look out. One of the horses was on the way up the slope with a big load on its back. But it had refused to go any further. It stood stock still with all four feet planted on the ground. The men pulled and dragged at the reins but the horse just whisked its tail and whinnied.

Then a huge fellow strolled up. "If you don't understand the ways of horses you'd better learn the ways of men," he berated them. And before the horse could raise its head to utter another angry neigh the man had grabbed hold of its hindquarters and lifted it off the ground. Then the horse trotted on as if it had been stung in the rear. Everyone around slapped their thighs and laughed.

"You certainly have brought an amazing company with you," said Aud. "Such feats will long be remembered here." She gave Brede a straight look: "But I realized some time ago, you know, that you'd given a space to slaves on board your ship!"

Brede wrinkled his brows. "I don't owe much gratitude to the earl," he said. "He and his Vikings harried and plundered along the coast for years. More than once he was after my little farm at home in Norway. Why should I say no when some of his slaves wanted to get away from him on my ship? Besides, the earl is dead now."

"All the same, you did play a trick on the earl's family there, Brede. Norway and Iceland aren't so far away from each other as you think."

"That may be," said Brede. "But Una and her brother Vidur are relations of my wife. I've always wanted to help free them from slavery."

"But what about this giant Digralde, then? They say he's been on a Viking raid with the earl, and that he's a great warrior and Viking."

"Digralde is like a lamb in bear's clothing," said Brede smiling. "But it's true that he has been out on Viking raids. That led to the earl setting him free, so now his fingers itch to get hold of some land and his own farm. He and Una have a child, a little girl who was born when there was a bad year in Norway. The earl ordered the slave child to be put out for the wolves, but Digralde had the child brought over to a farm here in Iceland, in a settlement further west."

Aud turned to the window again and looked at the crowd outside. In the midst of all the people she caught sight of two red-haired slave children who were struggling to drag a heavy chest along.

"Brede," she said sharply, fixing him with her eyes. "Those two Irish slaves...You aren't minded to give them their freedom too?"

Brede stroked a groove in the tabletop. "I've always thought that free people work better for their master than those who are not free, actually" he said softly. "But I expect I'll need them on the farm for a while. My two old slaves aren't fit for a lot any more."

"Well, you've always had a mind of your own, Brede. Even to marrying someone from slave stock too."

"I have a good wife in her," said Brede. "I've never had occasion to object to the way she ran the farm. She was lovely, too, when I first set eyes on her. It's four generations since anyone in her family were slaves."

"But she does come from a slave family," said Aud.

She rose and set her belt and linen head kerchief to rights. "Well, what I would say to you, kinsman, is that you should never take it for granted that the earl's folk won't seek revenge. Ossur Svarte, who is the headman in the neighboring settlement here, is uncle to the earl. Therefore I advise you to send Digralde and his people away as soon as you've built your farmstead. In the fjords to the west there are people from many parts of the great world, Celts, Faroese and Hebrideans. You can be sure no one there would ask about his family."

"Thank you for the advice, dear kinswoman."

"Take good heed of it," smiled Aud. "When they call

me Aud the Wise, it isn't because I let my tongue run away with me when I give advice."

∼

Brede took land in the north of the valley. He rode toward the sun with a flaming torch in his hand, shouting: "Here I claim land, for no one lives in this place. Hear this, spirits and trolls, you who live in mountains and rocks. This is my land!"

Brede had managed to bring some timber from Norway. The rest of the farmhouse would be built of stone and turf and driftwood that had been driven by wind and waves on to the coast of Iceland. He dreaded starting in on the work now, in the cruel wind and gales, with snowflakes fingering his neck. Although the winters in Iceland were milder than Norway's, the wind howled right through marrow and bone.

"Oh, pooh." Digralde spat on his fist. "It's no good going round rattling bones here." He started off on clearing the site of the farmstead. First a little wall had to be built to the south, so the foundations were level and strong. Reim and Vidur and Brede's three sons took part in the work.

They stayed at Aud's farmstead that winter. Tir was freezing cold day and night. She slept with the other slaves in the stone building where the animals were kept.

"I never expected to spend the last part of my life away from my homeland," said old Fulne, the oldest of Brede's slaves. He had a leg of mutton to gnaw, but it was slow work, for he hadn't many teeth left. He slurped his drink and smacked his lips and peered from beneath his Grey tufts of hair as he spoke. His wife, Trane, stood stirring the soapstone pot with a long wooden ladle. The scent of newly cooked broth floated through the room.

"They say Brede likes women and good food better than the sword," grinned Fulne. "But that's been a good thing for us. He's not one of those who makes free with his stick."

Trane laughed a hoarse little laugh. "It may well be he has a bit of respect for old Trane. You must remember I have been with him since he was born. And I suckled him for three years. That's why he grew into such a strong fellow. But now he can't get much help from his old slave woman any more. It's a good thing he's got some strong new slaves."

Reim yawned, sitting on the floor in front of the hearth: "I don't want to be a slave any longer. I want to go back to Ireland."

Fulne laughed. "You may as well forget such ideas, my lad. I have never heard of a slave who went back to his homeland. I myself was born on Brede's family farmstead. He inherited the smallest farm and the oldest slaves when he went and married Bergliot against his father's will. I've never had the chance to know freedom. And what I don't know, I don't long for either."

Fulne threw the mutton bone out through the narrow window and wiped off the fat on his coarse tunic. "I hope all goes well for Brede here in Iceland," he said. "We have been through many hard times together. We've sown and harvested year after year, chopped timber and built new houses. There was bear hunting too when we were at home in Norway. Yes, Brede is a fine fellow. There's just one thing he wants to keep for himself, like other farmers," he chuckled. "Nobody is allowed to touch his horse. If he could choose, I think he'd rather sleep with his horse at night."

Sote whinnied. He seemed to chuckle and agree with what Fulne said. But Tir was glad that Brede stayed with his family. When darkness fell over the farm she crept close to the horse's warm belly.

~

The biggest farm in the settlement belonged to the chieftain, Gissur Lodinsson. Gissur came from a great family that had moved from Norway to Iceland almost a hundred years before. They had taken a great deal of land and set boundary stones beside cornfields and pastures. The farmstead was magnificent. It was unusual to see such fine untrimmed timbers in the farmsteads of Iceland settlements. All the doors in the house were decorated with carvings in which dragons and fabulous animals twined around each other.

Gissur had two sons; the eldest named Gorm, the other Grim. Now and then the chieftain's sons came riding through the settlement on their lively horses. They went down to the cove where the longships were kept. The young people gathered down there. The lads from the bigger farms went around measuring up the ships and chatting about how they would soon be old enough to sail. Gorm had relatives in Norway and was going off that year. Grim was staying at home. He had a matter to put before the Ting, the assembly.

When the chieftain's sons rode by, the poor people lined up to take in the impression of festivity and color for a brief moment. The young men wore such fine clothes. They had shoes of soft calf leather that were laced round the ankle. They had jackets of the finest, thinnest woolen fabric, silver belts round their waist, golden buckles, golden thongs round their stockings, and cloaks bordered with leather. They were like a flock of proud hawks circling round each other stabbing and clawing wherever they went. They compared notes on swords

decorated with silver and copper, and ran their fingertips over shining spear points. When they couldn't decide who owned the most splendid weapons they rode to a level stretch of grass, just beneath the mountain. Here they fought each other in single combat. But often such battles led to many years of hostilities.

Ravn, Brede's son, admired the chieftain's sons. But he kept his distance. He was always fearful of being reminded of his lowly birth. In Norway he had been derided more than once because his mother came from a slave family. It had burned into his bones. But one day I'll show them, he thought. One day I'll show them what I'm made of, even if I don't have the blood of chieftains in my veins.

~

"Do you remember the stories Grandmother Gaelion told us," said Reim. "About the fearful dragons that spat brimstone and fire at Christian folk?"

Tir laughed. Did she remember? They were so frightened that they hid themselves right under the blanket on

Grandmother's bed. But they begged for more all the same.

"I've seen a dragon like that," said Reim. "I have seen it here in Iceland."

Tir's eyes were wide. Her spindle fell down on her lap. "What's this you say, Reim? You must be ill."

"I say that I've seen it with my own eyes," said Reim crossly. "Do you think I'm lying?" He frowned under his red forelock.

Tir grew thoughtful. He could be quite jittery, this brother of hers. He could jump out of his skin merely if he heard the cat mewing in the dark, and he pressed close to her if they had to cross the farmyard in the dark. All the same she didn't really believe what he said about the dragon. There was so much between heaven and earth human beings couldn't understand.

"Where did you see this dragon?" she asked seriously.

"Just behind the mountain in the north. I ran over field and hill to catch Sote who had gone trotting miles away. Then it suddenly happened. I heard a hissing sound, and then down in the ground it started to bubble and seethe. A poisonous yellow vapor drifted over the field. I gasped for air.

Then the dragon came. Its head was hidden behind the drifting vapor, but I clearly heard how its nostrils snorted and blew. Suddenly it sent a foaming gush of water straight up in the air. The water poured down all over me and I was soaked to the skin. But before I knew it the dragon vanished again and sank down into the bubbling, seething ground. Then I threw myself on to Sote and galloped off. I thought the troll hags and mountain spirits were grabbing at me with their porridge ladles. The gust of heat followed me a long way."

Tir shuddered. Then all the talk about this land must be

true. Iceland was a perilous land for people to live in.

"I'll never go near that place again," said Reim.

Tir made no reply. Anything dangerous and exciting attracted her in a strange way. She might well dare to go there some day or other. Little did she know the day would come sooner than she expected.

⁓

From Aud's farmyard they could look down on Ingolf's farm. It was made up of a cluster of turf houses that seemed one with the ground. Just then they heard laughter and noise down there: a crowd of children ran after each other among the houses. After them sounded an angry woman's voice calling them indoors: "Helga," she called, "Ivar, Stig, Endre, Kjellaug, Njål..." She called out a whole string of names, and children came running from all directions around the corners of houses, and vanished through their mother's doorway.

The first time Ingolf came over to greet Brede he brought five of his youngest children with him. They crowded around their father the whole time, crawled up on his lap and tugged at his beard. Two boisterous twins ran around teasing the dog so it jumped about and barked furiously.

"Ugh, all those kids," said Bergliot, laughing helplessly. "Times were certainly not peaceful in the old country, but I'm not sure there wasn't more peace and quiet there, all the same."

But no one could deny that Ingolf and his wife, Vigdis, were good helpful neighbors. They had lived in Iceland for almost twenty winters, but they remembered clearly how they had struggled to begin with. They often came over to see if there was anything they could give a hand with. Ingolf had a lot of good tools for both building and carpentry, and Vigdis brought some carded wool for Bergliot to spin. That would be most useful when the loom was put up in the new farmhouse.

Among all Ingolf's children Tir had noticed a freckled, merry girl with fair hair and eyes as blue as the sea. She was Helga Ingolfsdatter. She often went riding on her little horse with its white coat, and she seemed to have grown together with the horse's back, she sat in her saddle so firmly. But most of the time she was busy with all manner of tasks on the farm. She went rushing to and fro among the houses carrying buckets and loads of hay for the barn. Her fair braids flew straight out in the wind.

One day when Tir was sent down to Ingolf's farm to fetch some tools she heard whistling and singing from the barn. Tir peeped in cautiously. Helga was in there chatting to the calves. There was a bent old woman there too. She was mucking out the cows with a wooden shovel.

Then Helga's little black cat came streaking out of the darkness of the barn. Tir stumbled over the threshold and fell on her stomach. She was unlucky, for she landed straight in the heap of muck the old woman had raked together.

"Oh, my," said Helga. "You chose the right spot there." She put her arms akimbo and looked down at the unfortunate Tir. Then she burst out into laughter that echoed around the barn walls. The cows turned and mooed. Even the old woman laughed with her toothless mouth.

"Here, let me help you." Helga picked up some straw and dried off the worst of it. "There," she said, "now there's only the smell left. But that will go off in time."

Helga took her by the arm. "If you like you can come and see my horses."

"I don't know..." Tir hesitated. Bergliot had told her to be quick.

"You can spare a moment, surely"...Helga pulled Tir along to the far end of the barn, where eight horses were tethered in a row. Only one of them was white. "That one is my horse," said Helga. "His name is Frostfur." She stroked and patted the horse's side.

"In the winter I sleep here just behind the horses," said Helga. "It's so nice and warm here. And then I'm not so frightened of the spirits either. There's such a rustling and swishing in the farmyard when the wind blows."

Helga pulled Tir over to a small pen. "The big sheep are out on the mountain today," she said. "But now you shall see one that's my very own." She bent over the partition and picked up a little bundle. It was no bigger than a ball of wool. "This little lamb was born much too soon," she explained. "But when she grows big enough I'm going to weave myself a fine woolen shift."

Tir laughed. The lamb was pink and puny, and had only just begun to grow little wisps of wool on its back. It bleated pitifully, wanting to be put down behind its mother's warm back.

"I do wish you were a slave girl on this farm," said Helga. "We only have old Drumba, and she's so old and horrid. But father decides. There are enough of us on this farm, he says, we don't want another slave to keep."

Tir was glad Helga wanted her company even though she was a slave. But at the same time she hurt inside. When they went out of the barn old Drumba was in the far corner. She stood there in her ragged shift and foot-cloths, and her eyes were dark and lifeless.

~

A few days later Tir met Helga again.
"Where are you going, Helga?"
She stood on the threshold of the barn as Helga rode

past on her little white horse. Helga wore a sheepskin jacket with a hood that almost covered her whole face. Her cheeks shone like fire in the bitter cold. She stopped the horse and laughed. Frosty vapor came from her mouth.

"Off to the pass to have a bath. Do you want to come? It's bath day today, you see. And you probably need to get some of that barn smell off, I should think."

Tir hesitated and looked at Helga doubtfully. Bath...now in the coldest part of the winter? No, that wasn't for her. Once, when she was in Norway, she had seen some Vikings run naked straight out of the bathroom and out to an open channel in the ice. They swam around there in the icy slush to harden themselves. They kicked up a din and ducked each other, and played up to the girls standing on land watching them. Helga had Viking blood in her veins. But Tir herself was Celtic, and didn't much care for snow and cold. She shook her head. No, this ice bathing wasn't for her.

"There's your household coming too," called Helga.

So they were. The whole party came riding along on their little horses; Brede in his heavy bear furs, and his wife Bergliot wrapped in a cloak bordered with wolf's fur. And Reim was there too! He and Ravn rode one of Ingolf's horses. Ravn urged on the horse. "Come on, gee up!"

"Get up behind me on Frostfur," said Helga. "We'll follow them. We're only going to our neighbor Snorre's farm."

The farm was not far away. When they got there Tir saw something she had never thought to see. The farmyard was covered with rough hoarfrost, but still steam rose from it. There was a spring there. A flock of naked children ran along the edge; they were laughing noisily and throwing themselves on their stomachs into the water, which splashed up on all sides. Tir shuddered.

Helga took off her clothes. "You come too," she said. "Come in and feel it. It's nice and hot!"

Helga's head bobbed up and down in the water. She huffed and puffed, spat out water and laughed. Suddenly she did a somersault in the water, but just before Tir thought she had sunk into the depths forever, she popped up again in another place.

Tir squatted down and dipped her hand into the water. She got a shock. What Helga said was right. The water was warm. Just the right temperature too...The same as it could be in the sea during the hottest summers in Ireland. It was pure magic.

The temptation was too great. She tore off her shift and jacket and slid cautiously down into the water. It closed around her body and the movements of the water felt like gentle stroking over her skin. But no one could make her stay in long. Deep down in the water there were sure to be both water sprites and dangerous creatures. She was afraid they would grab her and pull her down into the depths. But at least she was braver than Reim, she thought proudly. He stood on the bank, well away with the horses, and didn't even dare put his hand into the water.

"Helga," she said, as they rode homeward. "They must be powerful, the sprites and trolls who rule the ground in Iceland."

"Hush," whispered Helga. "Don't speak so loudly. There are eyes that see and ears that hear everywhere."

She stopped the horse and whispered: "Do you see that high mountain over there to the north? The old people say that long long ago, before the first settlers came to Iceland, the great powers who dwell in the mountain showed their anger. They say the mountain opened up and tongues of fire reached right up to the sun. There was a crashing and booming in the glacier, and the sky grew dark with a thick rain of ash. Huge boulders fell like hail over the plain and killed both animals and people."

"Just behind the sacred mountain," Helga went on, "that's where the troll hags make their witches' brew."

Tir realized that must have been the place Reim had talked of.

"Hold on tight," said Helga, "we'll ride over there."

Tir leaned close to Helga's back. Shivers ran down her back when she saw the yellow vapor drifting over the

ground and heard the boiling and bubbling deep down in clefts and crevices.

"Listen to it rumbling down in the ground," said Helga.

Tir listened. The sound grew stronger. She clasped her hands tightly round Helga's waist. Suddenly a huge stream of water shot straight up out of the ground. It foamed and splashed around them. It poured down like a rushing white waterfall of boiling water and steam.

"Pooh to the troll pack," said Helga and spat. "We'd better get away from here. Trolls and spirits get so mad when people go near where they live. Old Drumba says there are more trolls than humans in this country."

Brede's farmhouse was coming on fast.

The children of the settlement stood admiring Digralde as he wielded a crowbar and heaved rocks out of the ground.

"You must be terribly strong," said Helga's littlest brother, spitting as hard as he could.

Digralde straightened himself and dried the sweat from his forehead: "Oh, well, I can wrestle a bit."

"How strong are you then?" asked another of the brothers, looking at the big fists and back muscles of the freed slave.

"Oh, I can probably pick up a horse if I get hold of it properly."

The youngsters gaped. Was it true? That he could lift a heavy horse!

"Well, a small one anyway," said Digralde with a chuckle.

One of the children braved going closer: "Is it true you've been on Viking raids to foreign lands?"

"It is true," said Digralde and sat down on the rock he had just pulled out of the ground.

"Was it exciting?"

"Oh yes, to start with I thought so. I got a tingling in my chest when I stood on the prow of the dragon ship with other men armed ready for battle. We sailed over the wide sea and came to towns and villages we had never seen the like of before. We stormed in with shining weapons to burn and plunder and rob them of gold and precious things. Then we sailed our bold ships off again and hid ourselves in the sea mists..."

The smallest boy pushed up the sleeve of his jacket and clenched his small fist right under Digralde's nose. "I'm quite strong too, Digralde, just you feel!" His eyes shone. "When I'm big I'm going to be a Viking too and go out on raids!"

"You certainly are strong," Digralde smiled. "But if I were you I'd use my strength on something better."

The children were surprised to hear Digralde say that. "The warriors are great heroes," said Ivar, another of Ingolf's boys. "Father says so. Once he went on a Viking raid to England. And Grandfather told us about warriors who fought and plundered in the far south of the world. They all won gold and honor."

"Ah, yes, how brave they are," said the smallest boy, sighing.

Digralde looked at them with his little watery blue eyes. "The warriors kill and plunder and burn down the farms of peaceful folk," he said. "I can't see what's so brave about that."

"What do you mean by that, Digralde?"

"Perhaps we didn't think much about what we did when we were out on raids," Digralde went on. "But later on pictures of it came before my eyes. I saw the faces of young and old screaming in terror. I saw little children trying to run away. I saw strong young men struck down. I saw girls and boys, no older than you are now, taken prisoner and dragged on board the ships."

Ivar scraped the ground with a stick. "Pooh," he said, squirming. "Couldn't they defend themselves, then..."

"They didn't have the chance," said Digralde. "We were strong. We had sharp weapons. The others were defenseless. They had nowhere to flee to, for the Vikings had burned down their farms."

"Have you killed anyone, too, Digralde?" whispered a little girl who stood fingering her braid.

"Yes," said Digralde quietly. "And that is the heaviest burden of my life..."

"I think I'll stay in Iceland," said Ivar when he met Ravn on the way home. "It can't be such fun after all, going on Viking raids like the grown ups say."

"What makes you talk like that," said Ravn. "You should just hear the Vikings talking about it! About strange lands where it's raining golden treasure! About houses with towers adorned with gold, about markets with wares from all over the world..."

"But Digralde says..." said the boy.

"Poof, Digralde! Digralde is happiest when he's grubbing in the ground like a pig. Someone who has been a slave for over twenty years doesn't know any better. No, Ivar Ingolfsson, just you wait till spring comes!"

Then the sun began to shine. It was like a new miracle every single year.

"D'you think it's true that the sun is made of pure gold?" said Tir.

"I think so, yes," Helga nodded. "There are dwarfs inside the sacred mountain who have forged it. If you don't believe me, just ask old Drumba. She knows all about such things."

Brede stood in the doorway of his new farmstead.

"In a few years," he said, "then you'll see I've really become someone! Then, when I drive the sheep home in the autumn, the whole mountain will seem alive there will be so many sheep in the flock. I'll send rolls and rolls of homespun across the fjord. Yes, the ships will be so laden they'll almost sink under the weight."

He laughed and watched the little snow-white lambs leaping around and playing in the newly grown grass. "Grow big and make your wool thick, little fellows. I'm going to need a new warm jacket soon, too."

Bergliot had been standing in the doorway listening to all her husband's chat. Now she put her hands to her sides

and laughed scornfully.

"A new jacket doesn't make itself, husband dear. It's not enough to hang a handful of wool around you and call it a jacket. You have to find someone to make it for you. I don't know who'll do that. I can't think of anyone."

"I'll give you a handful of wool," Brede chuckled. "If you don't behave I'll exchange you for a sheep. That'll be just as useful." Then there was uproar in the house. Brede gave Bergliot a slap on the place where she was broadest, and then they chased each other right through the house. Bergliot could give as good as she got. She rushed over to the cooking pot hanging over the hearth. She seized the ladle with both hands and slung some of the porridge right in her husband's face. It stuck there in a big lump in the middle of his shaggy beard.

Their big sons sat on the long bench laughing. They all understood why their parents behaved like children. There was a good smell of newly hewn timber, three cows and twenty sheep grazed just outside the door, and up to now they had not been troubled by illness. Their first months in Iceland had gone well.

Then Una and Digralde made ready to go westward. "I can't rest till I see our little daughter again," said Una. "She'll probably have taken her first steps by now."

Digralde laughed proudly. "I'll wager there is no bigger and stronger girl in the whole of Iceland. I'll bet my front teeth she can run faster than a deer already."

Una packed up her possessions in a bundle: a steel to make fire with, a spoon and some bone combs, and then a shawl Bergliot had woven for her. Vidur only had a knife, which he stuck in his belt. But everyone was interested to see what Digralde was taking. On board ship he had guarded his sack as if it had been his treasure chest. Now he loosened the string and thrust his hand inside it. "Look," he said to everyone standing around. "Here is a fistful of earth."

"I thought it was gold you had in your sack," said Vidur, roaring with laughter.

"Gold!" Digralde snorted. "No, no, a fistful of earth is more valuable than all the worldly goods and gold in the world. I've never seen anything sprout and grow in gold. This is the soil of our homeland! I shall spread it on the field the first time I sow corn here in Iceland."

Ingolf had called in at the farmstead. He stood looking at the melt water from the glaciers rushing down not far from the farm. "It's a perilous journey you're starting out on," he said, "past stretches of sand dunes and wild water-falls."

"We'll be careful," said Una. She took Bergliot and Brede by the hand. "We shall never forget what you have done for us. Now we feel like free farmers."

Then they set off. They did not have any horses, so they had to go on foot. But there was not much more than two days' march west to the fjords.

~

Helga thought up so many funny things. She was always full of sudden ideas and pranks. She had a wooden stick she called "Hummer." She bored a little hole in it and fastened a long leather thong to it. Suddenly Helga would come running down the hill with Hummer waving in the air. She turned it round and round with all her might till it made a low humming sound. Then the horses took fright and ran off at a gallop. "But that didn't much matter," Helga thought. "As long as it was only the neighbors' horses."

Helga was seldom alone. Usually she carried one of her younger brothers or sisters around. The little twin girls were always at her heels. One day when Tir was down at the stream fetching water, Helga followed her.

"Now I've managed to trick those little pests of mine," she giggled. "I climbed over the roof of the sheep shed and then ran as hard as I could over the field. Ugh, I'm so fed up with them. They pester me all day long, and at night I have to share that narrow sleeping bench with the twins."

They began to haul and drag at the buckets. Beside a big rock they stopped to rest.

"You're never angry with Reim, are you," said Helga

quite crossly. "You're always in a good mood, you are."

"Oh, no, I'm not," said Tir. "Back home in Ireland I could often be like a hissing cat–Reim can tease something dreadful."

"But now," she said, hesitating a little, "everything's different. Now there's just the two of us. We never seem to disagree about anything any more."

Tir grew thoughtful. How was it going with her little sisters, Moira and Cara, and little Roderick? If only they had been here now she would never grumble at all at them even if they pounded her black and blue.

Helga chattered on: "Father says they have a different religion in your strange country. And some of the merchants say there's a great House of God there, much bigger than Chieftain Gissur Lodinsson's house."

Tir nodded. "Our farm was just beside a monastery. And in that monastery lived Brother Cormac."

"Brother Cormac?"

Tir laughed and grew really merry.

"Yes, you should have seen Brother Cormac come rolling over the farmyard to taste our good plum wine. Then he could be quite light on his feet even though it was hard to understand how his legs could carry his huge stomach. We giggled and hid ourselves in the tall grass. But Brother Cormac could always find out our hiding place. He had a hooked stick he caught us round the neck and pulled us in with. "Rascals," he said, sounding gruff. "And you're supposed to be Christian folk!"

Tir told Helga about the little village in Ireland, about the miller and the parish priest and all the children at the neighboring farm. She talked about the red apples in the monastery garden, about the secret cave up on the mountain, about the rides in the meadows and Stella the little gray foal.

"That was when we didn't have slaves' names," said Tir. "We were called Patrick and Sunniva and our father was a free Irish farmer."

She stood up and picked up the bucket by its handle again. Then they heard a twig snap. Tir had learned to be careful after she became a slave. She bent down and peeped out from behind the bushes. Helga did the same.

It was a young girl they had heard. She drove a herd of cows in front of her. Her long braids danced on her chest as she hopped along from rock to rock.

"Why, it's my sister," whispered Helga, surprised. "If she wasn't looking so happy I would have guessed she was out searching for me for some boring job or other. What happened to her, I wonder? She looks positively giddy." Helga put her hand to her mouth. A half-strangled giggle came from her throat. Tir gave her a dig in the side: "Hush," she whispered. "Look, someone else is coming!"

Helga stared. "Did you ever see so many crazy folk out in the twilight? If it wasn't Brede's eldest son there too..." Helga went purple in the face with stifled laughter. The lad leaped along gaily, clapped his heels together as he ran, and uttered yells loud enough to make the moon jump. He was like a half-wild ox. With a great leap he joined the girl. He lifted her up and twirled her around. Then they both stumbled and rolled around in the heather. The cows stood around lowing and staring, they had never seen the like of such antics.

Now mirth came bubbling up in Helga. She clutched her stomach and curled her legs underneath her while she screamed with laughter. The two down in the heather looked up in fright and got to their feet again. Brede's son glared crossly around him.

"Come away," Tir whispered. "Kåre gets pretty mad."

They bent down and crept away from one rock to

another. Before Kåre reached the big rock they had vanished into the shadow of the woods.

"Weird that people can be such dimwits," said Helga, puffing. "Love, old Drumba says it is. It's a nasty sickness, for sure. She says it's worse than the plague even."

They chortled and laughed as they strolled down to the settlement. Not until they were back at the farmyard did they remember they had left the water buckets behind the big rock.

~

"Do you remember the great oak forests at home," said Reim. "They were really good for playing with bows and arrows!"

They were in Brede's hay barn. Tir closed her eyes. In her memory she saw the huge crowns of the trees in Ireland where the light played in branches and leaves. There she could walk along gentle paths with her face turned up to the green sky that seemed to arch over her and enclose her in a special secret world. The wind made the sound of the forest; rays of sunshine created the image of it. There was a rustle of life among the knotted branches, light shone in transparent foliage and dark green ivy twined around the tree trunks. The forest changed the whole time. She saw elfin faces peep from among the leaves, she saw fairy-like creatures dancing and swinging in the treetops.

The forests of Ireland belonged to archers and robbers. She played there with the children from the neighboring farm. She hid behind the thick trunks and trilled like a squirrel when they didn't find her. No one knew so many good hiding places as she did—in hollow oaks and the tops of the trees. No one was so good as she was at finding robbers either. Then she crept around with watchful eyes on every leaf that moved. On their backs they carried longbows and quivers full of arrows. "Look there," she would call, pointing to a shadow behind a tree. "There's a robber!" Then their arrows whistled off towards it at once, and they rejoiced in chorus.

Tir opened her eyes. They sparkled impishly. "What I remember best from that time," she said, pulling Reim's hair, "was beating you at shooting!"

"Ouch, let go of my hair! You can't hit an ox from just a foot away!"

Then she fell on him and they rolled around scuffling till the straw flew up in all directions. Laughing and out of breath they sat up and looked out of the barn door.

There were no big forests in Iceland, only a birch copse here and there. They were strange little stunted trees with twisted trunks and branches. The tough little birches clung firmly to the earth fighting a bitter struggle with wind and weather. This wood too had its own particular sound and its own colors. When the leaves rustled and sang in the breeze, or the water drops sparkled on the leaves after rain. They often played tag among the white trunks.

"Tir," said Reim. "We could make longbows for ourselves. It's a long time since we tried that."

She nodded eagerly and they ran out of the farmyard together. They found some flexible birch branches, and set to work at once. They shaped the bows with their knives, whittled arrow shafts and fastened small bone splinters in one end. They spent several evenings together on this work. Then they went out to try the new bows. They chose a birch tree and drew their bowstrings. Swish, the arrows lodged in the trunk of the tree so they sang. Tir laughed and jumped around so her copper colored braids danced round her head.

Soon some of the other children on the neighboring farms wanted to join the game. They met at sunrise and held contests in the meadow. When all Ingolf's children joined in they played hostile armies keeping watch over each other. They hid themselves in the thick brush and skulked around with their quivers on their backs. But Helga never managed to hide for very long. Suddenly they heard her chortling laugh behind a rock or a tree root, and then her red-cheeked face would pop up.

Brede stood in the doorway at Bredesgard watching the game. "It's entertaining to see puppies tumbling around at play," he said to Bergliot. "But there won't be much time for that when we are busiest in midsummer."

One day Helga's big sister came along. She walked with an angry tramping stride. She stopped in front of Helga threateningly, hands on hips.

"Hopeless child! Rushing over the fields and hills when there's work to be done at home. You've to come home and do carding, Mother says. The day will come when you'll regret not knowing more about the work on a farm! That's what Mother says."

Helga said nothing. She slowly turned up her face to her sister, smiling mischievously. "I know something about you, I do," she said slowly, "that no one else knows. Oh, yes, I know. I heard it from the troll in the big rock over there..."

The girl lowered her eyes. Even in the dim light they could see the blush spreading over her face. It wasn't easy to tell if it was from anger or embarrassment. She turned and went off without a word, her fists clenched.

"Carding is the worst thing I know," said Helga.

~

Ravn could carve runic letters. One of the chieftain's

sons had taught him how. They had sat close together under the shadow of the sacred mountain in moonlight.

Now Reim wanted to learn the art. There was power in runes. Runes could heal sick people and make them well. Runes could calm the storms and quench the flames licking over the roof ridge. If you mastered the art of rune carving you could be carried over field and hill, over land and mountain, through forest and pass, and go wherever you wished.

"If you teach me the art of runes you can have this sword," tempted Reim. He showed a little wooden sword he had been whittling at while he looked after the sheep.

Ravn snorted. "Father has promised me a proper sword as soon as I'm fifteen," he said. "I don't play with wooden swords like a trouserless baby any more."

"But do teach me about runes, won't you," said Reim.

"Runes and secret signs aren't for slaves," said Ravn.

But still, Ravn wanted to show what he was worth. He knew the Irish slave had talents he himself didn't master. One day Reim had brought out an old hide and a raven's feather he'd sharpened at one end. He dipped the point of the feather in the soapstone pot containing some plant dye Bergliot used to color woolen cloth. Then he'd started to scribble on the hide. He controlled the feather point with a sure hand and made the finest flourishes and borders in rows. "That's how I write in my tongue," he said. "Here it says: "Praise be to St. Patrick who protects the green island of Ireland." And then: "Deliver us from Vikings and robbers!"

Brede laughed, but Bergliot clapped her hands at the fine drawings. Now the hide hung on the wall of their small living room, in the center above the long bench.

"Come with me when the moon shines above the pass," said Ravn. "Then we'll go up to the sacred

mountain."

Reim's heart skipped a beat. He lay in the loft and peered up through the smoke vent until he saw the cold face of the moon rise above the hill. Then he went out into the farmyard. Ravn stood waiting behind the long wall. Together they went up toward the blue mountain outlined like a gigantic sleeping animal in the darkness of the night.

Ravn stopped beside a flat slab of rock just beneath the crag. They sat down there. Ravn dropped his voice to a whisper as he watched the clouds chasing over the dark sky. "It was Odin himself who taught us the runes," he began.

"Tell me about Odin!"

Ravn clasped his hands around his knees and moved closer to Reim.

"Great Odin swoops over sea and shore on his swift stallion. His black ravens fly around shrieking hoarsely about everything they see around the world. Odin knows everything and can do everything. He is the god of wisdom and minstrelsy, of fighting and war. When the winds howl, it's Odin out gathering in all the homeless ghosts..."

The wind swept over clumps of heather and dry stalks. From somewhere just behind them a bird flew up screaming from its nest. Reim huddled closer to Ravn.

"In order to gain wisdom," Ravn went on, "Odin sacrificed one of his eyes to the source of wisdom. Then he hung from a tree for nine days and nine nights while the wind howled. He sacrificed himself to himself! No human being can understand that. When he cut the rope and came down on the ground again he knew the art of making runes."

Reim shuddered. The racing clouds turned into ghostly figures riding through the air with flapping cloaks. All kinds of apparitions and specters must be out on a night like this.

"Now, look at this," said Ravn, taking some pieces of wood and a knife from inside his jacket. He began to carve the wood. "The first letters of the runic alphabet run together into a magic word. FUTHARK..."

"Futhark," Reim repeated. He hardly opened his lips.

"This is how you write your name!" Ravn scratched on the wood and showed him. Then he engraved runes with strange shapes. Steam in the flames, fire in the sea...

They were secret words whispered from ear to ear. No one spoke them aloud. They had to be engraved on wood and stone and on sharp weapons. The rays of sun and moon must not light on the runic signs.

"We have to sit like this for three whole Thursday nights," said Ravn. "Not until then can you learn the art of runes."

Tir knew nothing of all this. She came upon Reim as he sat engraving his bow. "What are you doing?" she laughed, peering inquisitively.

Reim was full of himself. "I'm marking my bow and arrow with runes," he said. "See what I've done here?" He held up his quiver and read: "Reim owns this."

"Reim owns this," she nodded. "That's smart. Now we shan't get our bows and arrows mixed up. And all the arrows that don't reach their mark will have your name on."

Reim snatched at her braid and pulled it. But Tir knew what to do. Reim's neck was so ticklish it took no time to make him let go.

~

One evening when Tir went out to the pasture to bring in the sheep she found Helga in floods of tears. She lay over the back of the biggest sheep and dug her hands into its fur, sobbing loudly and heartrendingly.

"Helga," said Tir cautiously, putting a hand on her head. "What's making you so terribly sad?"

"I've lost my freedom," sobbed Helga. She turned up her tear-drenched face to Tir. Her eyes were swollen with weeping.

"What!" cried Tir in dismay. "Have you become a slave too! How did it happen, Helga?"

"You don't understand anything," screamed Helga, thumping the poor sheep's body. "A slave like you...If it had only been no worse than that. I am going to be married!"

Now Tir sat down on the grass. It was a long time before she got her voice back.

Helga wiped her wet face with the back of her hand. "There's something I haven't told you," she said. "Perhaps because I wanted to forget all about it. I've been betrothed for almost a year. It happened last summer when I went to the Allting assembly with Father. It was there that he met Starkodd who lives in the fjords to the west. I bitterly regretted having nagged Father to take me to the Ting, because before I'd heard a word about it he'd promised me to that old man. Starkodd is almost forty winters old. And the only thing he thinks about is getting himself some heirs."

"But you're not much older than I am!"

"I'm fourteen summers. But Father is keen to get this marriage settled, so that Starkodd doesn't break the agreement. Father says he has a lot of children to think of, and he won't get such a good marriage for any of the others. Starkodd's farm is a big one, with hundreds of sheep and cattle. And he has big ships too that sail to other lands with homespun and feathers."

Helga began to sniffle again. "Father has decided that the wedding will take place just after midsummer."

"But what does your mother say?"

"Not much. Sometimes she strokes my hair and says I have such a clever way with the animals that she'll probably never get such a good shepherdess again. And then she comforts me and says: 'You'll be all right, daughter dear...' "

Helga hid her head in her hands. "Oh, it's so horrible. I want to run far, far away. Can't we escape together, Tir? Tonight!"

Tir didn't answer. She cuddled close to Helga. Below

54 them the fjord was calm and blue, shining with rays of light from the sun that was sinking into the sea. The sea, she thought. The sea was like a rocking blue melody singing about her homeland. Only the sea lay between this land and her own. But the sea was so enormously vast. It had taken three weeks to sail from Norway to Iceland. Then how many days would it take to get all the way to Ireland from here? If only you could climb on to a bird's wings and fly off, with land and sea beneath you right over to the green island in the southwest...

Tir glanced at Helga, sitting with her hands clutched tightly around her knees. She couldn't imagine Helga as a married woman...Helga with her freckled nose and childish blue eyes, Helga who sat playing with her wooden dolls behind the sheep pen. No, she couldn't see Helga as a housewife on a big farm.

They sat together there for a long time. Helga hiccuped after her weeping. Hiccuped and hiccuped while she struggled with herself. Then she stood up and straightened her shift. "Come on," she said. "Come on, all you lambs of mine. This is the last summer I shall spend as a shepherd girl at Ingolfsgard!"

∼

The next day Helga was her old self again. She seemed to have a special way of shaking off all her worries. After sunrise she joined the others in the forest with her bow on her back. She wanted to take part in the shooting match.

They were so taken up with their game that they didn't notice the riders approaching the meadow. Not before Tir took hold of Reim's arm and said: "Look, the chieftain's sons are just behind us."

Reim turned round quickly. Four or five lads sat there,

each on his white horse. They wore blue and brown
cloaks edged with leather, and golden belts round their
waists. They all had swords, and wore golden ribbons
around their foreheads. They sat on their horses proudly,
watching the game.

Now they called to Reim. "Who are you, so clever with your bow?"

"I am Patrick," he replied. "I'm Irish. In this country I'm called Reim."

"Then you're a slave," the other said. "No free farmer's son has a name like that."

Reim bowed his head. He was used to giving way before the chieftain's sons. He had learned to do that when he was a slave in Norway.

"But I'm sure you don't shoot as well as Grim Gissursson," said the biggest of the boys, jumping down from his horse. "It would be fun to try to draw my bow with you. See that bird up there? Let's see who can hit it first."

Reim's fingers started to tremble. He would have liked to get out of this. But he felt he had no choice. The chieftain's sons held power. He was only a slave.

He drew his bow and shot. The arrow sped skywards but didn't hit its quarry. Straightaway Grim sent off his arrow. But he didn't manage to reach the bird either.

Then Reim's fingers suddenly gained strength. He put an arrow to the bowstring and aimed long and precisely. The bowstring quivered. The arrow flew whistling through the air. There! It struck the bird, which fell to the ground just at the feet of the chieftain's son. Helga laughed in her merry way, and couldn't stop herself from exclaiming: "That was a master shot, Reim!"

The other lads nodded in agreement, but Grim's eyes filled with anger.

"Let me see your bow," he said.

Reim passed him the bow.

Grim drew the bow and aimed at a bird flying high in the sky. This time he struck lucky. This time he escaped words of scorn from the other chieftain's sons.

"Your bow is a good one," said Grim. "You can't be much good as a slave, you're so small and feeble. But it's plain you know how to make bows."

He swung himself up into the saddle. "You can soon make a new bow, slave. I've got more use for it than you, I'm going out on a Viking raid next summer."

Reim ran after the horse for a while. There were tears in his eyes.

"Poof," said Tir. "That's nothing to get worked up about. It was just a bow and a few arrows..."

Chapter Two

Isn't Reim coming soon? Tir wondered. She must have been asleep, for she felt so stiff and strange. She shuddered a bit when she saw how dark it had grown around her. Down at the ship they had lit some torches that threw a red glow of flame over the sea.

Senses alert now, she strained her ears for the sound of a whistle. But she could hear nothing but the sounds of the sea beating on the shore and the wind playing with the leaves in the low birch wood. What if Reim didn't come, the thought struck her suddenly. What would she do then? She couldn't turn back and couldn't set out on her own. The thought frightened her so much that her whole body seemed turned to ice.

Be brave now, her beating heart whispered. She had had to say that to herself many times during the past few years: Be brave, show you have Irish blood in your veins. You can't depend on others; you must rely on yourself.

Then came a cracking of twigs somewhere in the wood. She

jumped. This time if it wasn't Reim, it might be people sneaking around in the darkness, longbows at the ready. Or it might be...She trembled. This country was full of trolls and spirits. She knew they were creeping around her now. Creeping among rain-wet leaves and slippery branches, beings with the nature of the forest and the colors of the forest. They grabbed at her with hands like knotted branches. They blew on her with breath that recalled the rustle of the wind in dry grass. Weren't those eyes she could see shining over there in the darkness? She knew the people of the netherworld could turn themselves into all kinds of animal shapes.

Be brave now, whispered her voice. She took out the leather bag with the food, but even the newly baked rye bread Helga had given her didn't taste as it should.

∿

Iceland was home to all the winds. The wind came from the southwest and whipped the clouds over the sky. The wind came from the north and east, whistled in dry stalks and branches, piped around house corners and swept over grass and heather.

And how it blew out at sea!

Almost every day they went out in the boat Brede had brought on the ship from Norway. They rowed out of the bay and out to the furthest reefs, pitching and tossing. Their stomachs turned over when the boat danced like a small nutshell in the waves. Nowhere in the whole wide world were there so many fish as out there. They seemed to seethe and boil just below the surface. As soon as they cast their lines over the gunwale they could pull up one fish after another. The whole boat was full of wriggling fish.

To begin with fishing was almost an obsession with everyone who settled in Iceland. They were out there in the boats, both men and women, scooping up fish, and the children competed to get the biggest monster on their hook. Once Tir caught a cod that was almost as big as she was. She held on to her line grimly and Reim rowed with all his might to keep the boat from being swept out to sea in the strong wind.

"Just think if we'd really been driven out to sea then," Reim said afterwards. "Imagine lying at the bottom of the boat running with the current and the waves for days and nights. That would've been exciting."

The fish were put out to dry on flat stones in the little bay just below the farm. Brede talked of building a boathouse for the little boat down there, and a small hut to hold nets and fishing gear.

Fish was everyday food at Bredesgard. Bergliot made a thin gruel to go with it. She was careful with grain to begin with in the new country.

The four slaves kept to themselves in one corner of the living space. They shared a big wooden bowl and ate with their own spoons. As the eldest, Fulne ate first. It was horrid to watch him dribbling into the gruel while eating. But both Tir and Reim shut their eyes and got the food down. In Norway they had experienced what it was like when the harvest was bad. They remembered all too well how hunger could play havoc with men and beasts. They were always afraid it might happen again.

～

"Father," said Brede's youngest son. "Gorm is going out on Viking raids this summer."

Brede sat beside the hearth whittling a piece of wood he was making into a plow. The wood chips made a heap of little round shavings on the floor. He didn't look up from his work as he said: "Ah, yes, I know these young cocks. They like to ruffle their feathers."

"Gorm means to go as far as Frankland," Ravn went on. "Folk say there's a wide river there that goes far into the country. There's great store of wealth along the banks of that river, especially in the gods' houses of the Christians—heaps of gold and silver treasure. And then there are great market towns there, where folk sell all kinds of wares, spices and precious carpets, pearls and sparkling stones, carved bone objects and drinking vessels of purest gold. There the people are clad all in silk and furs. They have so much gold and jewels they positively glitter, folk say."

"You got your tongue going in a big way, there, I must say," mumbled his father. "But luckily we've got no use for such fine things. Overmuch gold would be a heavy weight to carry for those who work the land." He went on whittling the wood. Then he held it up before him, peered at it and said: "D'you think this will be a good plowshare, my son?"

Ravn went to stand in front of his father. His eyes shone: "A lot of people in the settlements here have grown rich and powerful after going out on Viking raids. They've won goods and gold and many slaves..."

His father growled: "Well, well. It may be they lose more than they win, these wild ones. At best they lose their lives, but some lose both arms and legs, and some lose their wits as well. No, boy, don't stand there in the middle of my heap of shavings!"

Ravn skipped aside, ashamed. He stayed scowling at the gray head bent over his work. His father was still straight-backed, and his powerful fists looked as if they could crush stone. During their past life in Norway he had been a great bear-slayer, the bravest man in the district, people said. He remembered the last time his father came home from bear hunting. The heavy, shaggy animal was slung over Sote's back: the spear was still stuck in the animal's body. His father led the horse by the halter, his hands were bloody and his face ripped by the savage claws. The farmyard was a lively scene. The dogs barked when they caught the pungent smell of bear and people came running from all the houses. They chattered excitedly to each other. What a huge monster! That was a real killer bear. And Brede had dealt with it alone, with no one to help him except his old slave. Ravn had been proud of his father then, so proud that his heart felt it would burst. But look at the doughty bear killer now! Now he sat whittling shavings and could be moved no more than a boulder in the field.

Ravn paced up and down. Then he stood before his father again, taking care to keep well away from the heap of shavings this time.

"Gorm says he needs more crew for his ship," he said in a low voice.

Brede filed the plowshare and ran the back of his hand over the wood to feel if it was nice and smooth. He laughed: "Yes, it's easy to get people to go on these excursions. The less sense they have in their heads the more courage they have in their hearts, those puppies."

Ravn grew red in the face. He bit his lips. "I'm almost fifteen winters now, Father."

Brede swept up the shavings with his hands and threw the whole heap on the fire. It burned straight away and lit up the whole of the little room. A huge shadow arched itself behind the farmer's back. His eyes had turned black.

"I can see you are serious about going out on these raids, boy. As if we haven't enough to do on the farm for years and years ahead! Who's going to plow the land, break in the horses, and who's going to build the house while you run around like a reckless warrior down in Frankland? Maybe you think the fields will sow themselves, the cows squirt milk into the bucket and the sheep come home from the mountain and put themselves straight into the soup pot! Now, my lad, it's about time you woke up!"

"But you have the slaves, Father, to do the work."

"Slaves, slaves!" Brede snorted. "As if it's the slaves who are to inherit the farm! No, anyone who's going to be a farmer must get to know the land before he can think of voyages of adventure. Viking raids are only for chieftain's sons and other sluggards who can't be bothered to bend their backs over the plow."

"Gorm's going to set sail as soon as it's full moon, Father."

"Then we'll be quit of him at last here in the settlement. There's not much joy in his staying at home as long as he thinks of nothing but bickering and starting trouble. It'd be best if we were rid of Grim as well, that power-mad brother of his. And mark this, my son: as long as I'm master of this farm you are to listen to what I say. There'll be no voyaging for you for the time being!"

~

Helga stood in the doorway of her house. "Come along in," she whispered, "come and see my wedding things!"

Tir crept inside. Ingolf was taking his afternoon nap after a hard morning's work in the field. His snores echoed around the walls. Some of Helga's little sisters sat playing on the floor, but they kept still as mice while their father lay on the bench. The elder children were with their mother in the barn.

"We must go into the closet," said Helga. They tiptoed across the floor and went into a small dark room at the long end of the house. Helga held an oil lamp which threw a pale flickering light over roof and walls. "Look, here are all the chests in a row!"

A chest with iron fittings and two more with wooden nails stood in the corner. They looked shabby and poor enough. Helga dropped to her knees, opened one of the chests and took out a whole bundle of colorful bands. They shone in blue, red and green. "Here are the bands Mother and I have woven on the loom!" She held up the lamp so Tir could see. Tir stroked the beautiful patterns with her fingers. She could weave bands too. Grandmother Gaelion had taught her when she was six years old. "You must work at your weaving so you have something in your chest when the time comes," Grandmother had said, winking slyly. "Suitors can come along before you've time to think about it!"

Helga opened the other chests: they held yard after yard of gray homespun. Her mother had spun the cloth during the long winter evenings. She had many daughters, so she needed to sit constantly at the loom.

"And look here..." Helga's face was bright. She opened the iron-fastened chest. In it were pots and frying pans and many ladles and scoops used in cooking. "I really know a whole lot about the work on a farm," Helga boasted. "I can bake bread, make broth and cheeses, I can spin and weave and make clothes. Yes, Starkodd is getting quite a wife, everyone here says so. And d'you know," she smiled broadly, "Father's promised me a pair of lambs for my dowry. I can choose the ones I want. But the best thing of all is that I can take Rimraggen with me."

Then Tir saw that Helga's little wooden doll was in one of the chests. "Are you going to take your doll with you too?"

Helga was embarrassed. The happiness in her eyes

faded. "Except for my lambs and Rimraggen I don't know anyone on Starkodd's farm," she said, looking down at the floor.

～

Tir remembered she had been very frightened of savage wild animals when she was in Norway. The winter after the crops had failed she had seen wolves sneaking like gray shadows over at the edge of the forest. Large packs of them had gone right into the farmyards that lay close to the forest. At one place the wolves had tugged at the jacket of a little boy playing outside the storehouse door. The people on the farm had to beat the beasts with spades and sticks to get rid of them.

She had never seen a bear when she had been tending the earl's cattle. But she had talked to many slave children who had met the bear. With terror in their eyes they'd told her about the great shaggy creature that came swaying along on two legs before launching an attack on its prey.

She was always scared stiff when she tended the cattle in the forests in Norway. The eyes of beasts of prey shone beneath the dark spruce boughs. There was a rustling and swishing in the heather and bracken. The huge moss-covered boulders looked like bears' backs. There was a tale about a little slave girl who had been torn to death by a bear.

There were no savage animals in Iceland. The sheep grazed on the great meadows that stretched away as far as the eye could see. They were out summer and winter in all kinds of weather. She'd never seen such big flocks of sheep as there were here. When the biggest farms gathered their flocks together it looked like an avalanche of white sheep's backs down the mountainside. It could be hard to keep the flock together, and quite often the lambs strayed away on the mountain or trapped themselves in a crevice. But there was never any need for anyone to be afraid of bears or wolves. Looking after the sheep in Iceland was a pleasant job.

Tir let her spindle sink down on to her lap. It smelled of summer everywhere. Of the springing grass, of sheep's wool, of the good warm earth. Brede had sold his ship and got himself more than fifty sheep instead. Some of the lambs were so small that Tir had to lift them over a stream or up a difficult stretch of hill. They trotted after their mothers, waved their little stumps of tails and brayed feebly and pitifully. She kept her eyes on them as they grazed peacefully among buttercups and grass down on the plain.

She folded her arms behind her head. Above her was the wide blue summer sky. The clouds sailed along in the light breeze with shapes like the strangest creatures. A big bird circled around on strong wings high up there. It might be a sea eagle or a hawk.

Then she suddenly remembered it—the fairy tale about the blue bird. It was as if she glimpsed Grandmother Gaelion's face among the light clouds. Her white hair lifted softly in the wind.

"Once upon a time," came her whisper, "there was a dainty little princess who sat spinning gold thread, as princesses usually do. She lived in a golden tower, and outside thirty of the noblest knights in Ireland kept guard, with swords and glittering helmets. For a wizard had foretold that one day she would lose her freedom and that no one would be able to rescue her without saying the right magic words.

"Suddenly one day a cloud passed across the sun and the sea grew cold and gray as steel. A rumble of thunder came from over the hilltop. Lightning and a flashing rain of sparks tore the sky.

Then a horrible big dragon came in sight. Its huge jaws gaped wide. The stream of sparks rose high in the air and scorched trees and bushes all around the castle. The knights fought bravely but their swords snapped like twigs against the monster. In the end the dragon got hold of the princess. It seized her in its claws and went off far to the north—to a land where the sun never shone, where the fields were covered with ice, where the snowstorms raged, and where beasts of prey howled in the gloomy forests. There the dragon took the princess, for there it kept a huge secret treasure trove of gold it had hidden in its stone castle.

As they approached the castle the princess heard weeping and wailing. It came from the many children the dragon had taken prisoner. The dragon had ordered them to weave a great carpet for his hall. It was to be black as sorrow and red as blood with pictures of all the evil to be found in the world.

The princess wept and prayed to no avail. She was made to sit and spin and weave from morning when the daylight seeped in through the small slit windows to night when darkness fell over the castle again. She wove, spun thread and wove again. She was almost blinded by tears all the time.

But no struggling warriors, or distress and suffering appeared in her weaving. As she wove a wonderful blue bird came into being. The princess was amazed, but at the same time she was in such despair that she hid her face in her hands and trembled like a windblown leaf. She was terrified about what the dragon would do to her when it discovered the bird.

Then a strange rushing sound began to fill the air. And

when she looked up she saw the bird had risen up from the carpet and was flying and circling above her head. It sang in a beautiful voice: "I have been sent here by the people of Ireland. I hold freedom in my strong wings. For a whole year we have searched for the magic words that would give you your freedom. We searched in the clouds, we searched in the forest, we searched in the pond. Then we searched in the eyes of a little Irish boy. And there we found the words that brought me here. Climb up on to my back, and we will fly away from this cold land of ice."

Then she felt the breath of the dragon. It stung her skin like glowing fire. There was thunder and rumbling in the air, and then the huge jaws came in sight over the hilltop.

"Hold on tight," twittered the bird, "hold on tight to my wings."

The dragon sent sparks and clouds of sulfur straight up in the air. Even the clouds burned like tongues of fire. But the bird flew faster than the south wind itself. Higher and higher it rose into the air. They flew through snow and dense fog, through freezing hail and wind. Then the princess remembered what she had missed all the time she had been a prisoner in the castle. "Where is the sun?" she called. "What's happened to the shining sun?"

The moment she spoke the words, heaven and earth seemed to tremble. The gates of the stone castle collapsed with an enormous roar, and suddenly big and small pieces of gold started to trickle out through the gates and the window slits of the castle. It was the treasure the dragon had watched over! The pieces of gold whirled round and round in the air and turned into a huge shining sun in the sky.

Then the dragon shrank down and disappeared with a huge roar into the sea, for no dragon can stand the sunlight. But the children came streaming out of the castle in hundreds—out to freedom and the golden light.

Now the bird carried the princess far across the sea all the way to Ireland. There the people of Ireland stood waiting. Their jubilation rose with a rush towards her, and all the bells in the town rang out. But joy shone most of all in the eyes of a little boy sitting high on his father's shoulders. His eyes shone like the summer sky itself.

Tir gazed up at the drifting clouds. She floated into the blue eyes and into the dream.

~

She woke to the sound of someone calling her name. Reim came running up the slopes. He waved and hallooed. "They're coming," he shouted, gasping for breath. "They're coming now!"

"Who are coming?" Tir had to laugh at his face, red with excitement.

"The bridal procession!"

Tir rose to her feet in a rush. She trotted after Reim up the little hill where there was a view over the settlement. It was true! There was the whole procession of wedding guests. They rode horses with fine harnesses, and they rang bells and waved colored banners. The women wore bright blue and red dresses with pearls and gold ornaments on the bodices. The men were just as fine in their white linen shirts with colorful jackets and silver mountings on the swords in their belts. There were some children too. Tir gazed and gazed at the pretty little girls sitting on their horses so proudly, with flowing hair and ribbons around their foreheads. How fair and beautiful they were! The cloaked man in the center of the procession must be the bridegroom himself. He was a tall fellow as bald as a coot but with a vigorous reddish brown beard. It looked as though he hadn't gone short of both meat and mead, for his stomach wobbled up and down as he rode.

The procession neared Ingolf's farm with noise and din. Ingolf was out in the yard waiting to greet the bridal procession. But Helga, the bride, was nowhere to be seen.

"I'm glad I'm not in Helga's shoes today," said Tir.

Reim tried to laugh a bit. "To think anyone could freely choose that rampant ox!" He nudged his sister: "If you'd been in Ireland now you might be married too."

Tir snorted. "I'm never going to be married. I'd rather go into a convent."

"But you sat there weaving faithfully and busily enough so you'd have something in your marriage chest. Don't try to deny it."

"Probably because everyone else was doing it..." She stood still for some time fingering her braid. Then she said slowly: "It was as if I thought we'd always be living with Mother and Father and our brothers and sisters..."

He nodded and looked down. Yes, he also thought the same thing.

They seldom talked about the farm back home in Ireland. It was easiest like that. For they knew old Fulne had been right. They'd never heard of any slave getting back to their homeland.

They walked back to Bredesgard in silence. The wind sighed over the pastures. It nearly always sang the same song. It sang of what it felt like to shake oak crowns and ivy, sweep over the thatched roofs and play with wild flowers and grass on St Patrick's green isle.

~

Helga sat on the cross-bench inside the dwelling house. She was dressed in festive colors, mostly red. That was the color of happiness and love. Drumba had combed her wiry curly hair until it was smooth and shone like silk under the light. This was the last time she could have her hair hanging loose down her back. The day after the wedding she would have to wear a kerchief like other married women.

"Raise the beaker, Helga!"

Helga held up the mead horn. She could just make out Starkodd behind the dense smoke rising from the hearth on the floor and out through the vent in the ceiling. He sat in the middle of the long bench among his wedding attendants. He was red in the face and the fat from the leg of mutton he was eating ran down his cheeks and beard. Just then he raised his horn and poured the mead down his throat. "Now, wife of mine," he shouted over to her. "You're getting a rich and powerful husband. Just ask for anything you want. I can't grudge you a gift on a day like this!"

Helga sat silent among her bridesmaids. Everything in the room seemed to go round and round. The visitors sang and bawled, and servant girls and slaves ran to and fro without stopping, with dishes of meat and horns of mead. Her little sisters and brothers had gathered around the fireplace and begun to dance a long-dance. They came in sight up and down amid the sea of smoke like strange underwater creatures.

Then she caught sight of old Drumba. Her crooked back was bent over the steaming pans of meat. That's how she had stood at Ingolfsgard for a whole generation now. Once her back might have been pliant as a willow branch, thought Helga. Once she might have gone running quickly and lightly across the farmyard—when she was young and had been brought over from Norway as a slave. Or had Drumba always been so listless and heavy? Most people born to be slaves were like that. They had no past and no future.

"Raise your horn, Helga!"

It hadn't been easy for Drumba here at Ingolfsgard. She was the only slave on the farm, and it was a hard slog to cook and wash for the household and thirteen children. Helga had an unpleasant memory. Once her father had beaten Drumba with a stick. There was no water in the buckets when he came in from the fields, thirsty and hot. He struck her, and her old back was more bent than ever when she picked the buckets up and ran down to the river. "That was a mean trick, Ingolf," her mother had said. "We have only one slave. You should be careful with your property!"

Now the drinking horns were raised again.

"Drink a toast with your husband, Helga!"

Strange, her thinking of ugly old Drumba just now. For she belonged to the farm just as naturally as the horses in the stable and the sheep out in the fields. Hunchback, they'd called her...

Helga stood up. Her cheeks were red from the mead. "There's one thing I want," she said in a loud voice. "And that is a slave that's mine alone."

Starkodd laughed. "That's not a difficult wish to fulfil," he said. "There are plenty of strong young slaves on my farm. Choose whichever one you like."

"I'd rather you sent one of your young slaves here to Father's farm," said Helga. "Father needs one. I want to take Drumba with me."

Starkodd laughed. "She can't be quite all there, your daughter," he said, and slapped Ingolf on the shoulder. "She could have had any of the gold I have in my chests, and all she asks for is an old hag of a slave. She knows how to make a joke, my young wife does. But everyone says a good laugh brings a long life, and that's no bad thing for a man nearing his half-century.

As soon as the wedding was over the ships set sail. Starkodd was off on a Viking raid, just as he used to do in Norway. He took sixty men with him on board his three ships. Young Gorm Gissursson, the son of the chieftain Gissur Lodinsson, set off in his ship as well.

Tir and Reim were out on the farm from where they had a view over the bay. Terrible memories always came back to them when they saw the dragon-like ships. Ships like that had sailed in to the coast of Ireland when they were taken prisoner by the Vikings and carried away as slaves.

The chieftain's sons had equipped themselves with coats of mail, helmets and sharp weapons. A crowd of small boys watched their brothers admiringly. "It's only five summers till I'm twelve," said a little freckled boy. "Then I'm going out to win land and fame. Look at their fine helmets, Mother—look at the sharp weapons. I'd much rather go with them on Viking raids than sit getting bored home on the farm. I shall go out and loot a whole chest full of gold and riches."

"There are riches enough in two strong arms, my boy," said his mother curtly.

"Women always gabble the same things," said the seven-year-old, spitting forcefully.

"Who says that?" his mother asked.

"Father does. And Grandpa too."

In the evening Bergliot went and called Ravn. She wanted him to help with some work out on the farm.

"It's odd I can't hear him answer," she said. "Have you seen him anywhere, Reim?"

"The last time I saw him he was with Ivar down at the bay where the ships were setting off," said Reim.

Brede looked up from working on the plowshare. He threw down his knife and stood up abruptly. "If that's the case," he said, punching the beam so the whole house rattled— "you don't need to go on calling, Bergliot. No matter how loud you shout now, only the wind can hear you."

~

The place seemed empty after Helga left. Tir missed her laughter and their games among the houses on the farm and out in the field. While Helga was there she'd hardly noticed how much there was to be done on a farm. Now came a time of long days and heavy work.

They spent the summer preparing for winter. Many days were spent in gathering produce and supplies around on the mountainsides. Brede and old Fulne went in front with the scythe and the others followed, raking the grass into small stacks. On other days they were out digging peat. They loaded up Sote with peat and took it home to the farmyard. There it was left out to dry in sun and wind.

The women were busy with dairy work. They made cheeses of goats' milk, and churned butter. Never had the cows given so much milk as that first summer in Iceland.

Every day Brede went out to the cornfield to see how

the grain was ripening. He shook his head at the clouds sweeping over the hilltops. "Now it's going to rain again. Cold wind and rain give no good harvest. We'd better get a sack of corn when the ships come from Norway with a cargo."

At the time when the mountainsides were in full flower, old Fulne died.

"He wasn't much good at the end of his life," said Brede. "But nothing would have brought me to rob him of life before his time, as many do with old slaves."

Both he and Bergliot mourned Fulne. At his funeral they buried his old bone comb and a small soapstone bowl with him. But the family on the farm took good care that this didn't get around the settlement.

⁓

That summer Tir felt her dreams and longing were stronger than ever.

The longing came over her when she hugged the warm bodies of the sheep or stroked the muzzle of one of the horses. Then she thought of the calves and the little lambs and the gray foal with the white star on its forehead. She saw them before her as they ran around the lush meadows in front of their little farm at home in Ireland.

The longing came when she saw the children tumbling around playing down on Ingolf's farm. How are my little brothers and sisters, she wondered? Do Moira and Cara still have their long braids? And little Roderick, does he have his new front teeth?

The longing came when she saw old Trane sitting with wool and spindle in the corner of the sheep shed. Grandmother Gaelion always sat like that in the evenings. Then the last rays of the sun fell on her silver-white hair and her hands twisting the thread with deft fingers, round and round without stopping. Out of everyone on the farm she probably loved Grandmother Gaelion best.

The dreams and longing came over her when she saw the ships setting off over the sea. She saw how the water sparkled, the sun-bleached sails cracked in the breeze and the prows plowed through the waves at great speed. Birds circled high over the mast. They followed the ships as far as they could over the glittering shield of the sea. She kept watching the birds until the beating wings lost themselves in the air and floated into the blue sea mist.

~

The time for the Allting, the national assembly, approached. Ingolf was going with his four sons and two of his daughters who were of marriageable age. Brede took his eldest sons and Reim the slave.

It was four days' ride to the place where the Ting was held. Rain fell heavily when they set off, and the mountains were veiled in thick fog. On the fourth day the weather eased, and the air was clear and warm with a blue mist over the bright birch forest. They had come to a broad plain surrounded by hills and mountains. A wide river ran foaming white through the cornfields and meadows. A steep mountain wall rose up in the middle of the plain. It was the Law Mountain itself, and on the level ground before it was the assembly place. There were people and horses everywhere. People who had journeyed from afar had built shelters with homespun walls, and there were so many little houses it seemed like a whole little market town at the assembly place.

There was an air of celebration when the Ting opened. A chief blessed the assembly and proclaimed peace for it.

As long as the assembly lasted no one must take up arms against another. Then the Law Speaker began to speak. He pronounced the laws in a loud clear voice. Around him the farmers stood listening with serious faces. Many cases were to be heard at the Ting, both family feuds and disputes between neighbors. All through the light summer night the hearing went on in front of the Law Mountain.

But many people had come to the Ting to meet friends among the settlers around them.

"Here is Farmer Brede," said Ingolf. "He's my new neighbor." He laughed: "Luckily no quarrels have broken out between us that need a hearing. On the contrary, there's to be a wedding next year between my eldest daughter and Brede's eldest son."

It was a great joy for Brede to meet up again with Asbjørn and some of the other farmers who had been on the ships from Norway. Now they'd all built themselves houses and were doing well in the new country.

The summer night was light and warm. No one thought of sleeping. Those who were not taking part in the proceedings under the Law Mountain strolled around among the houses. There were all kinds of things to see. Merchants stood outside their booths offering their wares. Some sold black falcons, some white fox furs and feathers, homespun and fine cloth, gold-trimmed belts and baskets woven with flax and horsehair. Brede went searching among the booths for he'd heard people at the Ting talking of a particularly clever blacksmith. Brede wanted to get his horse shod and also buy some small items for Bergliot. He followed the sound of hammer blows to the blacksmiths' booths.

Then they heard a growling voice. "Hey, stop there, farmer. Don't you need a safe lock for your chest? There are thieves and scoundrels everywhere."

Reim stopped abruptly. He'd heard that voice before. When he turned round he could hardly believe his eyes. Over there, beside a modest little booth, stood Digralde. He took up almost the whole opening with his heavy bulk. He had a sooty hide around his middle and held a pair of smith's tongs in his hand. The forge glowed and crackled as he heated the iron.

"Well, well, I never thought the smith I was looking for was an old acquaintance," laughed Brede, big-eyed with surprise too.

"They say there's something in being blacksmith to your own luck," smiled Digralde. "Last winter, over west in the fjords where I have my farm, the old blacksmith died. And so I thought if there's anything I'm good at, it's swinging a sledge-hammer." He brought out a smart little chest with a lock and key and offered it to Brede. "I don't like making weapons," he said. "No, I'm happiest as a locksmith." He laughed: "It takes a good head to make a good lock, not just strong fists."

Brede wanted to know how the others in the west were getting on. And Digralde told him. Vidur had signed on as crew member of a merchant ship—"he wanted to be free and take care not to bind himself to any young woman." Astrid grew more and more lovely every day. "She's getting more and more like her father," said Digralde with a merry glint in his eye. Una was fine too, but she'd grown strangely round in the stomach lately...

Reim was looking over at the booth next door. A young fellow there was selling gold buckles. A group of girls had gathered round him, and it looked as if the man was keener on joking with them than selling. He pinched their cheeks and winked right and left while twirling his fine curled moustaches.

"That fellow is Irish," Reim thought. "I'm sure he's

Irish. He's wearing just the sort of clothes people have at home in Ireland."

Digralde laughed. "I think I can read your thoughts," he said. He took Reim over to the trader.

"I don't want to disturb you, Bentein, when you're so well occupied, but here's a young man from your own country. I thought you two might have a few things to chat about."

Bentein smiled under the elegant moustache, and greeted Reim in Irish. Reim thought it sounded like beautiful music. It sang and hummed in his ears. It was the first time he had heard his mother tongue after being kidnapped from his homeland.

Bentein was not at all surprised to hear what Reim had to tell him. That sort of thing was almost a daily happening in the part of Ireland he came from. Bentein himself had come out of it well. And that was because the Viking women liked him so much that they looked after him nicely, he said, winking. Now he worked on a ship belonging to Chieftain Ossur Svarte as a trader.

"Do you go all the way to Ireland?" wondered Reim.

"I've just come back from there," said Bentein. "And I expect it'll be a long time before I get there again. You see, I have a sweetheart here in Iceland now."

Reim and Bentein stood there chatting for a long time. But at last Bentein packed up his things in a bundle. "I'm off to see if the ale wives over there have some good stuff in their booth," he said. But before he left he bent down and whispered into Reim's ear: "If we meet again, you know you can rely on Bentein. It's happened that I've managed to get Irish slaves back to their homes before now! But not a word about that to anyone!"

When evening came many people gathered at Old Gudmund's place. He was famed for being the best teller of tales in the whole of Iceland. Brede and Digralde and many other farmers were there too. They seated themselves in front of the old white-bearded man and listened to what he had to tell of the old clans in Norway. He told stories of wars and fighting and murder until cold shudders ran down the backs of his listeners.

Reim did not know much about the clans in Norway, and he couldn't understand the difficult names. He sat thinking all evening about what Bentein had said.

In the days that followed there was sport and games in the meadows around the Ting place, with tugs of war and leg-pulling and other amusements. No one could beat Digralde at such games. Folk gathered around him gaping in wonder as he had one fellow after the other on the ground. In that way he sold a lot of his blacksmith's wares.

But when the races began he packed up. "I haven't got a chance with this caper. No horse could pass the winning post first with Digralde on his back. Besides, a man who is going to be a father is as jumpy as a flea on a live coal," he laughed. But before he left he got to see some exciting horse fights. The animals were in an enclosure snorting and kicking. Two stallions were driven towards each other. They lashed out with their hooves so the ground shook. Around them stood a close circle of men who moved out of the way as the horses fought. "Go on," they shouted. "Bite and kick!" They laid bets with silver rings and coins on the horse they thought would win.

"I could do with another horse," said Brede. "Here in Iceland there are more horses than people on the farms."

The farmers exchanged words and smiled. Many of them wanted to show off the lovely little foals they had

brought to the assembly. Brede looked at eyes and teeth and felt the legs of the horses. A farmer from the neighboring settlement wanted to take him into one of the tents to bargain over a beaker of mead.

"I must watch out not to get drunk," chuckled Brede. "Or someone might cheat me into buying an old nag instead of a nimble little foal. And then wouldn't my wife Bergliot give me a thrashing!"

All the same, Brede ended up buying a horse from that man. It was a small, shaggy white foal with black forefeet. Then he went on to enjoy one and later two shots of strong mead, for of course he had to drink to the transaction.

"I suppose you couldn't use a slave as well," winked the man, giving Brede a friendly nudge. "I have a good example here." He pointed to a young lad standing by the opening to the tent.

"No, thanks," said Brede. "I've finished trading now. I have two strong young slaves and an old one at home. I'll manage with them."

"The horse races are starting," came a call from the sports ground. Ingolf made haste. His son was taking part in the race.

While the farmers chatted Reim went cautiously over to the slave boy. They stood looking at each other for a long time. In the end Reim plucked up courage.

"Are you a Norwegian?" he asked. "Or perhaps Celtic," he added, when the boy made no reply. Reim did not know any more languages. The boy just gazed in front of him with frightened eyes. It seemed most likely that he came from the land of the Arabs. He was dark-skinned and his hair was shiny and black.

He probably has a strict master, thought Reim. It's always worse being slave to a chieftain. He recalled his own time with the earl in Norway. There had been thirty slaves in the slaves' house there, and a slave-minder who kept watch over every step they took. He also knew that the dark-skinned ones who looked different from the Scandinavians often had to endure more blows and abuse than other slaves do.

"Here," said Reim, putting a piece of the bread Bergliot had given him into the boy's hand. "You probably need it more than I do."

The boy's face lit up. His eyes were like dark shining stones. He pointed to himself. "Amed," he said. That was his name.

More and more people streamed up to watch the race. Most of the riders were young fellows. The chieftain's son Grim was there, and many other leading men's sons. The horses snorted and kicked out, eager to set off. A strapping fellow with a long whip tried to keep the horses in a straight line.

Then the man raised his hand. The ground drummed. The horses leaped over the flat grassland. It was a wild ride. There were cries and ringing oaths when one of the riders lost his seat, fell off and rolled under the hooves. Ingolf strained to see. His son had reached the winning line. He was not up with the leaders but neither had he come last. It was just as everyone had expected. Grim raised his hands proudly in victory.

In his mind Reim saw himself rushing along on Stella, the gray filly at home in Ireland. She must have grown big now and certainly taller and more beautiful than the little Norse horses.

Suddenly he was woken from his dream by a sharp blow on his back.

"I've seen you before, red mop!"

Reim jumped. He looked straight into a cocky face with cold steel-blue eyes. His fair hair fell like a mane down over his shoulders. He sat high in the saddle of a restless bay horse. In his hand he held a stick he used for urging on his horse. Now Reim had felt the stick.

"How does a slave boy like you come to be here," sneered the fair-haired young fellow. "You must have seven league boots to cover the ground. Last time I saw you, you were the slave of my cousin the earl, in Norway." "Father," he called to a man in a cloak with black hair and beard. "Look at this slave here. He belongs to our clan, but hasn't the wits to stay at home where he belongs."

Reim shrank down and turned cold all over. As if in a bad dream he was back on the earl's farm in Norway. It was Christmas festival time and the chieftain's sons had been invited to the farm. "Look, there's a slave," they yelled. "Let's have some fun with the wretch!" They beat and tortured him till his stomach turned and everything went black.

Ever since that day the fear of meeting any of the earl's people again had followed him like a shadow.

"Who's your owner?" asked Narve, poking him with his whip.

Reim stammered. He couldn't get a word out. Luckily there was a call for the next race over at the racecourse. Narve smiled nastily and looked down at Reim: "We'll meet again, slave. Maybe by then you'll have learned to speak the Norwegian tongue!"

Then he rode off to the starting line.

Reim slipped away. His heart hammered so hard he thought it must echo in the mountains around the sports ground. He crept behind Brede's back and stayed there.

Now the sound of galloping hooves was heard again.

The riders stormed across the field. Dust rose high in the air as they rushed past.

Then they heard someone shout: "This time you'll meet your match, Grim Gissursson!"

"Who's the fair man in the blue cloak," wondered Brede.

"He belongs to the earl's family in Norway," said Ingolf. "He's to take over his father's big place here in Iceland. Narve is his name."

Brede kept his eyes on the bay horse as it rushed along with flying mane. It was a strong horse and well trained. It began to come up level with Grim's white horse.

Then it happened. Not many people saw it, for the dust-cloud hid both horses and riders. When Narve was about to ride past, Grim pushed against his horse's legs and held it back. The bay stallion lost its footing and stumbled, and Narve fell off headlong with his cloak over his head. Some of the spectators laughed aloud at the sight, but Narve raised his fist: "You'll regret this, I can tell you, Grim!" He swung himself on to his horse and rode off in a fury.

Reim felt glad Narve had something else to think about than searching for runaway slaves. He just hoped that the father, the mighty chieftain, would forget what had happened too. As they rode home from the assembly he turned his head cautiously to look for the chieftain's company. Then he caught sight of Amed tied up to the bay stallion. So he had been sold, then. But he was not going to a kind master by any means.

～

When they were settled in back at the farm they drove the sheep down from the mountain for shearing. For days on end they stood bent over the animals, wielding shears.

Ulla packed the fleeces in big baskets and Brede carried them away. Tir had to laugh at the cropped sheep's bodies. They stood there thin and blue looking in the strong summer light.

As soon as the birch leaves began to turn red and yellow it was time for carding and spinning. "If I put all the sheep who have given wool for the yarn I have spun through my long life in one place—well, it would look like a big white sea out on the field," said old Trane. "Sometimes I dream about it at night." Day after day she sat spinning with her hand spindle. The reel went round and round until far into the evening. She blinked her little shortsighted eyes when Tir sat down beside her on the bench.

"I'll probably be doing this work in the other world too, when I get there."

"Don't you need to rest, then, Trane?"

"Oh, bless you, no. I don't suppose a slave woman gets any rest either in this life or the next." She smiled her toothless smile. "Maybe Freya or one of the other goddesses will want a new dress. Then old Trane will have to sit at her spindle again."

Over in the closet Bergliot sat at her loom. She pushed up the weft with the reed. Bump, bump, bump, it went every time. She had to make use of the daylight before the days grew too short.

As she sat there her thoughts went all the time to her youngest son. Wherever he was in the whole of the wide world, she hoped all the gods of Valhalla would watch over him wherever he journeyed. She knew women in the neighboring farms who had never seen their sons again.

She pushed away the painful thoughts and bent over the piece of cloth that was to be a jacket for Brede. Life was strange. Now it was almost thirty years since she had

first met Brede. Her cow had run away, and she rushed after it down the hillside so her skirt and her braids flew out behind her. Then a young man came running along on the flat ground—he seized the animal round its neck and held on tight. There was a teasing smile hidden in his blue eyes as he walked toward her leading the cow by a tether.

Bergliot smiled. After that it had been just the two of them. They seemed to have caught the disease people called being lovestruck. But it had not been easy at first. Everyone in the settlement knew she had slave's blood in her veins, even if four generations had passed since anyone in her family had been a slave. Her grandfather had been given his freedom because he had served his master so well.

Brede was the youngest son on a big farm. She could still see his old father sitting in the high seat pondering on man after man who had followed each other for fourteen generations. It was not with his blessing that his son should marry into a slave family. The only person who had helped them was a relative on Brede's mother's side, the one called Aud the Wise.

There was a great deal of difference between free and enslaved people, thought Bergliot. But once in the morning of time the gods must have decided that things should be thus.

She glanced over at Tir bent over her spindle wheel. Bergliot felt sorry for her. She knew her own family had gone to Norway in the same way. They had been carried off by Vikings somewhere down in Frankland. That was why she had black hair and a dark complexion.

Bergliot pushed the last weft into the loom and rose to her feet stiffly, rubbing her tired back. "It's getting late, she yawned. "I think we're all dropping off."

Then she heard the cock crow loudly and shrilly. Bergliot turned her head and listened. "When the cock crows at this time of day it's a warning of fire," she said, shuddering. She raked the embers in the fireplace carefully together and sprinkled ash over them before creeping under her fur coverlet.

What Tir remembered most from that horrible day when she was snatched away from her homeland was the smell of burning. Sometimes she woke up in the middle of the night if the fire was smoking too much. Then she sat up with a jerk, and stared out into the darkness with wide-open eyes. She saw again the red flames licking up the tower of the monastery church. She saw the birds fly screaming up from their nests, saw how the crown of the great oak tree crackled and snapped before it swayed and crashed to the ground so the sparks shot high into the air. Then it took hold of the roof of the farmhouse. The flames gobbled up the straw thatch with terrific speed. The little room, the sleeping bench she lay on, her little wooden doll, her mother's loom, the fine chests her father had carved...all were devoured by the snarling tongues of flame. The smoke smarted in her eyes and nose.

Then something happened that made her remember the frightfulness and terror still more strongly.

She was on her way home with a flock of sheep that had strayed too far into the hills. The clouds hung low over the hilltops. She was afraid it was going to rain so she ran as fast as a hare over rocks and clumps of heather, driving the animals in front of her with a little birch branch.

Then she suddenly stopped and breathed in. She recognized the acrid smell of smoke that could not come from any bonfire. She started to tremble all over. There

was no doubt about it. It was the smell of burning. Dark clouds of smoke surged up on the north side of the ridge.

She ran up the nearest rise as fast as her legs could carry her. On the top she stood still to get her breath back. Then she saw it. Down in the valley the tongues of flame blazed high in the air. It was Chieftain Gissur Lodinsson's farmhouse that was burning. She heard screams and shouts from down there. Grownups and children ran about the farm like frightened animals. The smallest children clung to their mothers. Slaves and servants were driving the animals out of byre and stall. The cows ran everywhere and a little trouserless boy screamed loudly in terror as the ox came thundering along as if to trample on him.

There were people inside the burning house. They ran around in there picking up things and throwing them out through the doorway. Some carried chests and boxes between them. There was a well in the middle of the farmyard, and men and women were passing buckets from one to another to pour on the fire. But it was no more help than putting a few drops of water into the mouth of a huge dragon. The flames spread with terrible speed in the wind. On the north wall where the fire burned most fiercely, the men were using fire axes to try to stop the blaze. The flames started to come up through the thatch. Suddenly the men gave a great yell. They grabbed their axes and leaped away in a rush. The great beam that held up the roof broke in two and fell down in the glowing sea of fire so the sparks rose high in the air. Gissur's farm was past saving.

At that moment a clap of thunder came from over the hill, and the rain gushed down. Tir stayed where she was in the downpour. Her legs would not carry her. She sank to the ground.

Then a ripping flash of lightning lit up the whole sky. At the same moment the sound of horses' hooves thundered across the field and a rider rushed past not more than a couple of arms' lengths from her. His cloak fluttered in the wind, and his hair shone almost white in the lurid glare of lightning.

⁓

Everyone in the settlement kept on talking about what had happened. The fireplace in the farmhouse had been in the middle of the room, but it was the north wall where the fire had started. The wall was close to a steep mountain face, where no proper watch had been kept lately. The slaves had to suffer plenty of blows on their backs because they had not kept a careful enough guard. Gissur went around in a rage hitting out with his whip. But the slaves wailed at him, saying they had not seen any sign of strangers on the farm. The lightning must have struck the roof.

Aud screwed up her eyes: It's my belief that lightning was thrown by a human hand," she said. "There was a lot of fighting and murder among the big families when they were in Norway. It would be strange if that didn't still go on here in Iceland. They can never let go of the thought of revenge. If only they could stay on their farms in peace and stop going around with their swords always in their hands."

"Yes, that would be a good thing for all of us," said Brede.

On Gissur's farm the slaves were clearing up after the fire. One day a ship arrived with a load of timber from Norway. By the time the corn was ready to cut, the new farmhouse was almost finished.

~

Not long after the fire something awful happened to Reim and Tir in the forest.

They were tired after days of hard work when the men came home from hunting in the mountains. Tir had helped to divide up the meat that was to be dried, and Reim had worked with Brede preparing the skins. Now it was good to be out in the hills. The sunrays slid among grasses and stalks, the bees hummed and rustled in the tufts of heather, and the bushes were covered with juicy blueberries. Oooh, how good they tasted! They spent the whole day picking berries, and it wouldn't be surprising if more went into their mouths than into Bergliot's buckets.

"You look as if you've rubbed your face in a blueberry bush," said Reim, laughing with blue teeth. They carried the buckets between them and set off for home. They went across streams and marshes where bog cotton flowers fluttered like light snowflakes on slender stalks. The forest was golden and dusk-colored. The sun was on its way down.

Then they heard the sound of hooves on the ground. "Hush," said Reim, "someone's coming." He pulled Tir with him into the thick undergrowth. They sat still as mice and alert behind the leaves, following the cloaked rider with their eyes. He stopped on the level ground just in front of them and let his horse drink from a little trickling stream.

"By St. Patrick," whispered Reim. "If it isn't Grim, the one who took away my bow!"

The great man's son had hung the bow over his shoulder. The runes stood out sharply in the light-colored wood, and showed who was the rightful owner. Reim's body twitched. It was as if he wanted to rush up and grab the bow.

But Tir grabbed her brother by the arm. "There's another rider coming!"

They crouched down again. The rider stopped just a stone's throw from them. Tir put her hand to her throat to stifle a scream. The rider put an arrow to his bow and aimed in the direction of the place where Grim was. Now they saw who it was. It was Narve!

Then a twig snapped, and at that moment Grim turned his head and looked round. Swift as a deer he jumped aside and swung himself into the saddle. The arrow landed on the ground quivering, just beneath the horse's forefeet.

"You muffed your aim there, Narve," he called

triumphantly. "You seem to have a habit of sneaking round like a wolf in the night. It wouldn't surprise me if it was you who burned down our farmhouse!"

"You wouldn't be far wrong there," Narve shouted back. "But there's still no one who can witness to it at the assembly!"

Then he swung the horse around and rode away like the clappers.

"Just wait till the next crossroad," Grim shouted after him.

~

A cold wind swept over the turf roofs of the farmhouse. Bergliot was in a sad and gloomy mood. She walked about like a ghost. She did not seem to see the people around her any more.

In the evening she happened to be right down on the shore staring at the waves breaking white over the rocky islands. Her big woolen shawl flew right out in the strong wind coming down from the mountains and sweeping over shore and hills. She stood there until the twilight wrapped itself around her: until she turned into a gray form that blended in with rocks and mountain.

Tir and Reim were out in the Bredesgard farmyard.

"We've been in this country a whole year now," said Reim.

Tir nodded. It was two years since they'd been captured by the Vikings and made slaves. She didn't want to think about it. She hid the thoughts in the very darkest corner of her mind.

"Have you prayed to the saints?"

Tir sighed. Every morning when the sun rose and every evening when it sank into the sea she had sent a prayer to St. Patrick, the saint who protected the people of Ireland, that they might go back to their homeland soon. But up to now he hadn't heard her prayers.

Reim took something from the lining of his jacket. He shaded it with his hand so the rising moon should not shine on what he showed her. It was a piece of wood. Reim had scratched some strange signs in a crisscross pattern on it.

Tir felt a thrill go through her. The signs were runes. They held secret magic.

"Come with me," whispered Reim. "Come with me up to the sacred mountain!"

They ran up the rocky slope, over moss-covered rocks and thickets, right up until they came to the flat slab of rock where Reim had learned the art of engraving runes.

"Listen," said Reim, whispering so low that his words almost ran away with the wind. He pulled her with him behind the rock, so its shadow hid them. "Listen to these words:"

> *No sun nor stars shall shine,*
> *No fire be lit on the hearth.*
> *No corn shall grow in the field,*
> *No child be born of mother's womb,*
> *Before Patrick and Sunniva,*
> *Tir and Reim*
> *be carried over the sea*
> *and all the way to Ireland.*

Tir was freezing. She made a shallow hole in the ground and covered the rune stick with earth and moss. They looked into each other's eyes for a moment. It was as if all the air was filled with power. Then they started to run. As they turned into the farmyard a violent rainstorm whipped over the field. Thunder rolled over the mountains to the north.

～

Bergliot sat at her loom as Reim came running into the room.

"They say ships are coming from far out at sea," he shouted. "They're making straight for the fjord here!"

Bergliot tied her kerchief around her head and ran out of the doorway. She shaded her eyes with her hands. The autumn sunshine was so strong it sparkled like pure gold out there on the sea.

Then she saw. Far off the ships rocked like bobbing seabirds in the waves. Bergliot recognized the figurehead on the leading ship.

"Freya be praised," she whispered, "they're coming back!"

She ran into the room where Brede sat bent over his bowl.

"We must go down to the fjord." There were fiery red patches on her cheeks. "Our son is coming back..."

Brede was about to take a mouthful of mead. Now he let his arm fall. He gazed at her and his eyes grew dark. "You can go alone," he said. "I don't want to be the first to greet Vikings and violent men returning from their raiding. My back grew bent this summer because I had to work twice as hard while those young bucks were out enjoying themselves!"

Bergliot knew her husband well enough to realize it was no good asking him something twice. But she noticed his hands shook when he raised the horn to his mouth.

So she went down alone. Down the little hill and across the beach to the sheltered bay where the ships usually moored. People had already gathered there. She knew most of them. Most were women with sons the same age as the boy she was waiting for. It was as if their hearts beat in time with each other while they waited for the dragon ships to come in. The short evening seemed to last a whole year.

Then the ships headed into the bay.

"Have they all come home," called the women. "Tell us now!" Their eyes searched among men and boys dressed for war. Now they were coming ashore. The gods be praised! There was Ivar, and there were Tor and Leiv and Sigbjørn. Gorm Gissursson walked down the gangway erect and smiling. On his breast shone many golden jewels he wasn't wearing when he set off. His mother rushed to embrace him.

Bergliot clenched her hands against her breast. Her tears were ready to flow. Where was Ravn? Where was her youngest son?

Then they carried ashore five stretchers covered with red blankets. Starkodd Viking called out their names. Bergliot felt a shock go through her. Three of them were barely fifteen years old. "They fought bravely," called the Viking. "Now they dwell in Valhalla, in the kingdom of Odin."

Where was Ravn? Where was her bouncy little son?

There he was! Freya, thou good goddess, there he was!

He walked down the plank from the rail supported by two grown men. His cheeks were thin and his eyes shone like dark marsh pools in his deathly pale face.

Bergliot ran toward the boy. "You're back," she said joyfully, clinging to his cloak.

Then she gave a scream. The cloak fell aside. Where the arm that held his sword should have been there was just a stump, hanging withered from his shoulder.

~

It was a long winter at Bredesgard. Ravn lay pale and

bloodless on the sleeping bench. He did not want to talk about his Viking expedition, but in time they got to know what had happened:

From Iceland Gorm had first sailed to Norway, where he had relatives. There a large number of ships mustered, and at midsummer they set course to the south.

Ravn stood on the foredeck with Vikings who had been on Viking voyages many times before. They were power- ful men with faces as unmoving as granite. They wore steel helmets and coats of mail. When the ship put in to foreign coasts the older warriors stormed ashore first. They raised their axes high above their heads and yelled their fearful warcries. "Watch this," they said, if the young lads hesitated, "this is how you do it, boy!" Then they raised the axes and struck. There was blood on the ground. There were cries in the air.

Ravn kept thinking about what Digralde had said that summer. He had never imagined the raids would be so horrible. He hadn't given much thought to the foreigners as human beings before. Now he saw the terror in their eyes, he heard the despairing cries for help; he saw old and young dying every single day. These violent men were like a swarm of grasshoppers racing over the land; they devoured and wolfed

down anything eatable they found, they trampled down cornfields and meadows in their constant hunt for things to plunder, they set fire to farmhouses and carried off cattle. He saw boys of his own age taken prisoner. They were crushed together and bound back at the ship. They lay there moaning as the ship sailed on to fresh destinations. Gradually Ravn began to feel ill. He had trouble getting his food down, and sometimes he vomited over the rail. Several of the young lads had the same trouble. They tried to avoid the others' eyes. No one wanted to be a coward. No one wanted to show weakness. It was a matter of steeling yourself. Just look at Starkodd the Viking! On his own he killed all the Franks who barred the entrance to the god's house where there were so many treasures. Starkodd would have plenty to tell when he got home.

When Ravn set out he had nursed a dream of coming home with piles of gold. But the only thing he had managed to grab for himself was a golden brooch from the breast of a young woman. It was in a small Frankish village the Vikings had burnt. The girl lay on the ground and looked as if she was asleep, with her black hair flowing beneath her neck. A little line of red blood trickled down under her bangs. When he saw something glitter on her shift he quickly bent down and snatched the brooch. But later on he had not taken much pleasure in it. The cold metal smelled of death. He was sure it brought a curse with it.

When no one was looking Ravn dried his eyes with the sleeve of his jacket. "I don't want to go on with this," he thought, freezing with horror. The wickedness was like a rolling wave that dragged more and more people with it and grew in strength. No one dared to break away. He didn't manage to break away.

"If only I'd been strong enough," he wept, "so I could

manage to stand up in front of the whole horde of armed men and say: I won't join in with this!"

But he hadn't managed it.

By the fall they were homeward bound, and landed somewhere in the Irish Sea. They sneaked ashore as dawn was breaking and hid behind some high bushes. Then a string of horses and cloaked men came along the path just in front of them. The horses carried big chests.

"We're in luck this time," whispered Starkodd. "These are Christian men. I can see that by the white crosses on their cloaks. "It wouldn't surprise me if they've got gold and fine things in their chests! Come on, the gold will soon be ours!" He gave a high-pitched yell, and then the horde of armed men broke through the brushwood and threw themselves upon the peaceful company.

But what none of them had expected was that the peaceful monks wore chain mail and swords under their monks' cloaks. Now they turned round in a flash, threw off their cloaks and seized their swords. The axe blades shone in the sunlight. Like thick hail the arrows ripped through the air.

Then it happened. A powerful red-bearded armed man came rushing straight at Ravn. The sight burned itself into Ravn forever. The man was almost twice as big as he was. He looked terrifying as he raised his weapon to strike. Ravn leaped aside. But he wasn't quick enough. The sword sank into his shoulder and jolted his whole body. Then Ravn screamed so loud that he felt as if earth and sky shook. The pain and blood, the wild cries, the men rolling around on the muddy ground with gaping mouths and eyes starting out of their heads...And the terror! The terror seized hold of him with spear-sharp claws and gripped him fast.

He lay there unconscious and later sank into feverish

red days and nights. He moaned and cried because the blow had not finished him off at once.

"Get a hold of yourself, now," said Starkodd. "It's true fate has been cruel to you, lad. But thank the goddesses of destiny that you've still got one arm. I've seen worse injuries than yours."

～

Bergliot and Brede held a ritual for midwinter night. They slaughtered a sheep and spattered the blood on the pale timbered walls. The smoke rose to the roof and out into the cold starry air.

Brede's face was twisted: "Cursed be Odin, God of War. Cursed by the evil god who thirsts for blood and death!"

"Hush," said Bergliot, staring at her husband with horrified eyes. "Can't you hear him rushing over the roof with his ghosts? Can't you hear..."

"I make offering to the goddess Eir," mumbled Brede with closed eyes. "She knows all about the art of healing, about advice for illness and health-bringing herbs. Our son is alive and that is a great gift from Eir and the good gods in the Home of the Gods. But the winter is long," he groaned, looking over at his son's pale face. "If only spring would come..."

They waited. Four times the full moon sailed across the sky. And the spring came, like a wonder, and everything was different. The trees were full of buds, and the melt water from the glacier foamed past close to the farmhouse. "Look," said Reim, pulling Tir with him. "Come and see what's hiding in this little tree!"

Tir ran over to where Reim stood. She stretched her neck. There! There were four little spotted eggs in a small nest. "Don't touch them," said Reim. "If you do the mother won't come back to the nest!"

They stood there a long time admiring the eggs and listening to the birds singing up in the air. Then Reim suddenly gripped her arm and pointed west of the farm where the earth was newly ploughed and black.

"It can't be..."

Yes, it was Ravn walking down there. He had hung the willow basket round his neck. With his good hand he sprinkled the seed corn over the field. The grains fell like little snowflakes into the black earth.

Brede stood at the edge of the field. He stood with a straight back, with his head bared. Sowing corn was a sacred action. But never had he felt it as he did this spring day in Iceland.

Then came the time when the cows were about to calve. Bergliot walked up and down the room restlessly. A mournful mooing could be heard from the barn.

"You'll have to fetch some water, Tir, even though it's nearly midnight."

Tir ran down to the deep quiet pool in the stream.

"I don't like the moon tonight," she thought. "It warns of something bad." She looked down at the cold moon face reflected in the smooth water. She came to think of one of the stories old Trane had told her. It was about two children who went off one night with a wooden water tub they carried between them on a pole. Then the moon came out, magical and beautiful, and the children stood staring at it. They stared so long that the moon captured them with its power and imprisoned them, and the children disappeared along the shining rays of moonlight.

Tir shuddered when she looked up at the pale face of the moon. It seemed as if she could see both children and the water tub up there. She filled the buckets with water and started dragging herself and the buckets homeward. Bergliot had told her to hurry.

Then she remembered she had left her little steel for striking fire on the flat stone at the edge of the forest. Surely it wouldn't matter if she popped up to fetch it. She ran quickly over the field, found what she was looking for and put the steel under her shift.

Then she heard a horse neigh over the hill and soon afterward two riders appeared on the ridge. It couldn't be any old farm chaps out riding so late at night. In the bright moonlight she saw the leather-bordered cloaks and silver facings. It was Narve and Grim.

I must get away, hammered her heart. But then it hammered still more: No, no! If you run off now they'll catch sight of you straight away!

The riders halted, as if greeting each other, then came riding along the flat ground in front of the stone where Tir was hiding. Narve rode with a straight back. His profile was sharply outlined against the yellow face of the moon. In Norway he had been the handsomest budding chieftain anyone could imagine. Now he had grown even better looking. He was big and broad-shouldered and had a flourishing fair beard, even though he couldn't be more than seventeen winters old. The only one who came near to matching him was Grim, sitting on his horse just opposite him.

The two riders sat like stone statues in the cold night. When Grim finally opened his mouth the words cut like swords through the silence:

"I suppose you expected to knock me down from behind, you cowardly dog, as you usually do. What've you got to say now you've met me face to face?"

"I'm not afraid of your ugly face," shouted Narve. "Let's put an end to this single combat, then!"

Both of them jumped down from their horses. They drew their swords like lightning. Sharp blades flashed.

Narve fought with his weapon just in front of Grim's

eyes. He skulked wily as a cat just before it launches an attack on its prey. He was quicker than Grim, who was more like a big growling bear as he swayed around waiting for his opponent to attack. Then, suddenly, Narve raised his sword and struck with both hands. Grim ducked away and parried with his shield. It was cut through right down to the handle.

Narve seized the axe hanging from his belt. The steel flashed when he threw the weapon through the air. Then Grim screamed. Tir shut her eyes. The scream went through her like an icicle. She seemed to feel it crunch through marrow and bone. When she looked up again she saw Grim had a great wound below the knee, blood poured out. He staggered and leaned against his horse. Next moment Narve was there. He struggled to free his sword from the shield lying on the ground, so it would be ready to strike with.

Tir felt sick. An evil spell seemed to have been cast over the night. It was a grim, grim world she had been imprisoned in. And as if in a nightmare she couldn't get out a scream and she couldn't turn away. She was forced to look at everything that happened without being able to step in.

Grim sank down along his horse's flank. He held on desperately to the bridle as if it was his last thread of life. Now Tir heard him sobbing aloud. He was helpless. Narve stood ready to deal the deathblow.

Then it happened. Grim's horse raised its forelegs and began to strike out at Narve when he came at Grim with his flashing sword. Narve stumbled and fell flat on the ground. Now Grim had the upper hand. He seized his bow, set an arrow to it and aimed. The arrow rushed through the air and pierced Narve's back with a dull sound. A smile spread over Grim's face. He threw himself on to his horse and sped away.

"You're late," said Bergliot when Tir at last came in with the water buckets. "The cow will calve any moment now. I think there'll be two this time. It's tiring to cope with it alone."

But then she caught sight of Tir's face. "What's the matter with you, girl, you're white as flax and shaking all over!"

Tir couldn't get a single word out.

"You must have come across both trolls and dwarves, child," said Bergliot, hurrying back to the moaning cow.

~

Then came days of rain and mist.

Brede rode on Sote up to the mountain. In front of him rode Reim on Blackfoot, the little horse Brede had bought at the Ting.

It was strange how the weather had changed up on the mountain. Brede and his sons had been up there only a few days ago. They had fished in the mountain waters and gone home with both trout and salmon. Now the mist hung low over the mountains. The great mountain to the north was outlined against the sky, dark and treacherous as a troll. The black, rain-wet mountainside glittered.

"I can see something white far up the mountainside!" Reim pointed up the steep rock-strewn slope.

Brede shaded his eyes. The boy was right. Some little white creatures clambered around high up over there. They must be the lambs they had searched for during the past few days. It wasn't easy to find them in this mist and wind.

Reim jumped off his horse and began to run up the slope. He was light-footed and climbed like a mountain goat over rocks and mountainside. He stopped high up there and hallooed down to Brede. He waved both arms and pointed. Brede saw what he meant. He seized the rope made of horsehair—the strongest he had—and climbed up the mountain after the boy. The ground was slippery. Water trickled down clefts and cracks, bringing with it stones and gravel. He was out of breath when he reached the spot where Reim stood.

"The smallest of them has a hard job to climb up by itself," said Brede, shaking his head. A long way down a little lamb had got stuck in a crevice and could go neither forward nor back. It bleated pitifully and stared up at them with bright eyes.

Brede tied the rope round Reim's waist. "Careful, now!" He tensed his leg against a big rock and held the rope with both hands, so the veins on them swelled. "Be quick now, boy! This is a strain..."

Reim lowered himself inch by inch. He hung between earth and sky and swung to and fro until he got a foothold on the narrow ledge. "Now I've got her," he called from far down. "You can pull me up now!"

Brede hauled and pulled at the rope. I'm no youngster now, he thought. This is harder than I thought. He dried the sweat from his face when Reim came scrambling over the edge at last with the little animal in his arms.

But then he smiled and shook Reim's forelock. "I know you were scared to death, lad, but you certainly have got guts."

They gathered up the little flock and started for home: down the mountainside and across the lava plain with the icy cold glacier water. Reim held the lamb safe under his jacket.

"Master," said Reim softly. "What are the chances of a slave being freed..."

Brede was weary after a long day. "That's for the master

himself to decide," he said curtly. "Most of them never give their slaves freedom."

I'm sorry for the boy, thought Brede. They're a fine pair of youngsters, these Irish children. But there was still quite a while before they would grow up.

"Look, it's clearing up," was all he said. "The moon will be up before long."

~

Bergliot stood up from her loom and put the yarn into the wool basket.

Then she heard steps outside. Who can be coming here so late," she wondered.

Aud stood in the doorway. "Is Brede in?"

"He's out collecting sheep with his slave. I expect him home soon. But come inside. It's no good standing out there in the gale."

Aud's eyes were gray as steel. "Troubles are brewing," she said. "Didn't I say that carting those slaves over to Iceland would bring bad luck? They have been the earl's slaves and all they plan for is taking revenge on his family. Now Slave Reim has taken the life of Narve Jarlsfrende. He was found with an arrow in his back."

"That can't be true." Bergliot flopped down on the bench. "Reim was with us all day yesterday."

"Wicked wolves prefer to sneak around in the dark," said Aud. "This is going to be no light matter for us. Narve's father demands that the slave be hung and full amends be made for his son. But I don't believe he'll be satisfied with that. He'll want a life for a life. You'd better take good care of your sons now, Bergliot."

Bergliot turned pale. She grasped the edge of the table tightly and for a moment it looked as if she would collapse. Aud caught hold of her.

"There's something here I don't understand," whispered Bergliot. "How can they be so sure it was Reim who killed Narve. From what I know of the boy he's not especially vengeful or bold either."

"You don't have much time to think it over now," said Aud. "Narve's family will be here soon."

Bergliot called her sons in from the field where they were training the horses. When they heard what had happened they seized their axes and long spears and kept watch by the peephole just inside the door.

Then she called Tir. But no matter how much she called she got no answer.

~

Tir caught sight of Reim and Brede high up the mountainside. Reim rode first. He sat on Blackfoot driving the little flock of sheep before him with a long birch stick. As she drew nearer she heard him singing at the top of his voice. It was a merry Irish song about a man who had taken a drop too much of the good wine, and who mixed up horse and cow when he was going to ride home from the gathering. When Reim saw Tir he put his hand to his mouth and made a sound like a ringing horn. Obviously he was in a happy mood after finding all the sheep.

But what's the matter with you, Tir," he laughed as she stopped breathless before him. "You've been running as if you had the devil himself at your heels. Has something happened to Brede down at the farm?"

Tir gasped for breath. She had run so hard she felt her heart would burst. Her words came in fits and starts and disconnectedly as she explained what had happened. While she talked Reim's face changed. A swift shadow seemed to rush over his forehead. His eyes grew dark and frightened.

"We must get away," stammered Tir. "They've sent people out searching. Soon both men and horses will be here. We've no time to lose."

"But what about Bergliot and the others on the farm?"

They'll get help from Aud. She has sent men and weapons over to Bredesgard."

Reim still stared at Tir in disbelief. "Surely they can't think that I, an Irish slave, am to blame for Narve lying cold on the ground!"

"It's happened before," said Tir, and now she felt impatient, "it's happened before that a slave has taken the life of his master. I doubt if anyone would think it strange that someone who had been torn away from Ireland by the earl's warriors should seek revenge and take the life of the earl's people."

"But everyone knows I was at home with Brede the night it happened."

"The truth is the last thing people will believe," said Tir.

Reim started. Only now did he understand his position. "What shall we do?" he asked fearfully, looking around. Far away near the crest of the mountain the old slave woman on the neighboring farm tended her little flock of sheep. Otherwise nothing could be seen anywhere on the bare expanse of mountain.

"I've thought out what we must do," said Tir quickly. "We must go west. If we can only reach the dense birch forest it will be easier to escape. We'll manage it," she said to encourage Reim.

Now Brede had come up to them. He grew pale when he heard what had happened. "Aud was right," he said. "Getting mixed up in the earl's affairs has led to nothing but trouble for me."

He jumped down from his horse and spoke to Reim. "You're in mortal danger, boy. You must try to save your skin as best you can. The goddesses of destiny are parting our ways now, and we're not likely to meet again. But I want you to know that I've always thought of you two more as my own children than slaves."

Tir pressed close to Brede. She wept. "Say goodbye to Bergliot for us," she said. "Whatever happens I'll never ever forget you."

Reim watched Brede and the little flock of sheep as they went down to the valley. But he had little time to lose. He turned on his heel and ran after his sister over the stony ground. The bridle path followed gray rock walls and steep slopes right up to the mountainside itself. They followed it all the way until they came to a narrow cleft covered with dense birch forest. The branches stood out like runes in the pale moonlight. They stopped for a while and fought for breath. The heavens arched wide and dark over them and the stars twinkled restlessly in the strong wind.

Tir pointed westward. "We must get over to the other side of the valley. There's a river there, and if we can only cross it we are safe."

Reim nodded. He followed his sister. He had never been in this area before and didn't know the way.

They ran down the rocky slope and through a thicket of dwarf birch. The rocks were shiny and slippery after the rain and the branches scratched their faces. They heeded only the need to go on...

Then Tir stopped suddenly and listened. Trembling she peered out into the darkness. Did she hear the sound of horses? She seized Reim by the arm. She glimpsed gray shadows above the hilltop. Before they could sigh, horses and riders appeared, no more than a few stones' throw away.

"They've seen us!" She pulled Reim after her into the

shelter of a big rock. They lay there still as mice. Tir heard
nothing but her own heartbeat. It thumped in her throat
and palms. Hard, frightened beats. Reim shook like a
wounded animal. He was almost senseless with fear.

"Reim, what are you thinking of. Sit still!"

Before she could grab hold of him Reim had slipped out
of shelter and was leaping through the sparse wood. He
ran among treetrunks and rocks like a hare pursued by
baying hounds. Now arrows began to rush through the
air. Tir felt a smarting pain in her arm. One of the arrow-
heads had struck her.

From her hiding-place she saw Reim running zigzag
through the wood to avoid the rain of arrows. "The slave
scoundrels won't get far!" shouted one of the men. He put
a new arrow to his bow.

Men and horses had stopped right by Tir's hiding place.
To her surprise she realized the warriors had not discovered more than one runaway. The arrow that hit her had
been meant for Reim when he slipped out of the shelter
of the rock.

"Don't shoot!" came a shout from lower down. "We've
got him now!"

Tir's hands went up to her neck. Her throat seemed
knotted up. I must help Reim, rushed through her head,
or they will make an end of him. Don't be a coward, she
said to herself. You have Irish blood in your veins!"

But at the same time there was something holding her
back. I can't help him now anyway, she thought. If I wait,
I can run on and fetch help. She stayed where she was
behind the big stone slab. Her body became one with the
shadow. The men began to swear and threaten down
there. She felt she was being stabbed with knives when
she heard her brother scream and groan. Now they're
going to kill him, she wept. If only St. Patrick would hear

her prayers!

She crept cautiously out to see what was happening. Reim was tied arms and feet. He lay lifeless over the back of one of the horses. One of the men gave an order, and then the group set off in an easterly direction.

Tir lay behind the rock until she was certain no one would discover her. Then she stood up and stole bent double and silent as a cat from rock to rock. Then she straightened up and ran over the great lava plain before her. She ran and ran without feeling anything but the stones under her feet and the mountains around her.

She did not stop running until she felt her legs wouldn't carry her any longer. Then to her surprise she saw a little isolated barn just below the mountain. It was quite visible with a thatched roof reaching almost down to the ground. Now she recognized it as the place they had stayed in when they first arrived in Iceland. She looked quickly around, but couldn't see anyone nearby.

The stars had already grown pale in the east. Tir crept into the barn, found a sheepskin and fell asleep almost at once.

She woke up with her whole body hurting. To begin with she thought it was because the sheepskin she had pulled over herself was full of fleas. She sprang up from the bench and started to shake her hair and clothes.

Then she noticed her arm. It was stiff and swollen; she could hardly move it. The arrow had gone deeper than she had thought at first. Some of the iron tip might still be in the wound. She felt it even more when she tried to pull on her shoes. When she was about to tie the laces around her ankles her fingers felt numb and without feeling.

She crept up on the bench again and pulled her shawl more closely around her. If only she wasn't so thirsty. But she didn't dare risk going out in broad daylight. She'd have to wait until evening came to cool her throat in the fresh river water that ran just below the building. Luckily she wasn't hungry, even though it was a whole day since she had tasted food.

The thought of Reim plagued her more than the thirst. Her poor brother, he might already be dead. Despondency sank down on her like gray fog. She was alone, and she was frightened.

Perhaps it would help if she went to sleep for a while. Sleep was like a good friend spreading out the soft blanket of oblivion. She closed her eyes and slipped into a dark and silent room. Once or twice she gave a start. She thought she heard dogs barking far away. Another time the door hinges squeaked in the wind. Were they coming to get her? She struggled up again and peered out through the slit window. The sky had put on its nightly cloak and the moon was creeping up the blue vault.

Then it was she heard Grandmother Gaelion's voice whispering from somewhere in the darkness: "Never give up. You have the courage to go on."

Her head felt as heavy as lead and she had to fight to stand up. She moaned when she bumped her wounded arm against the wall.

Suddenly everything was clear to her. The forces of darkness were luring and lulling her to sleep in this lonely house. She must go on to save her life.

Outside the moon shone through the pass—a pale, wicked face over the hardened landscape. The mountains threw long shadows, and far up against the light night sky lay the glacier like an icy cold hand with fingers grasping at the valleys. There were no trees in this part of Iceland, only great boulders as if a giant sprite had played at throwing them over the valley long before the first human settlers had started to build in the country. Tir hid herself in the shelter of the rocks every time she heard sounds that were different from the whispering wind. Cold chills ran down her back when a loud scream cut through the silence. But it was only a ptarmigan that flew up from a thicket and sped on swift wings over heather covered stony ridges.

Her tears came with sobs as she ran along over stones and tufts. Her wound hurt so badly. She felt something wet and warm running from her shoulder down her sleeve. Her legs hurt too. The soles of her shoes were coming apart from the thin leather uppers. It was like running barefoot on the sharp stones.

But fear was the worst thing. It tore and dragged at her like a spear of steel. So they were going to end their lives in this pitiful way after all—as slaves in a strange country, as people with no rights. No laws could protect a slave accused of a crime. She knew what the punishment was...Death.

If only I get there in time, the thought coursed through her. She felt pierced in the heart whenever she thought of what they could do to Reim. Now and then grim pictures came to her. Reim had been punished before. She remembered his bloody back the time he had been shepherding the earl's flock in Norway. When she thought of that she was almost blinded by tears.

Then she recalled things from their time at home in Ireland. She remembered her father pinching her cheek and saying: "It will take more than a few storms to break you, my little wild girl!"

Her father had been right. She wouldn't give in before she had mastered the letters Patrick had learned at the monastery school; she wouldn't give in before she could shoot with bow and arrow as well as her brother. Once they had had a little calf that was so sick no one saw the sense of letting it go on living. Then she had begged to be allowed to nurse the calf. She had stayed with it day and night. She had never given up hope that it would recover. When the summer was over the calf had grown into one of the finest of all the cattle in the pasture. She was proud when her mother stroked her head and said: "You must be cut from the same cloth as Grandmother Gaelion, you know, Tir. She'll never give up once she's got something into her head."

And now, thought Tir, now that's more important than ever before. If all the powers of heaven stood by them, she would manage to save Reim.

She clenched her hands as she ran. It was more than half a day's ride to where she was going. But if she jogged along like this she might get there in time.

She stopped, gasping for breath. Then she heard a rushing and roaring far away. And when she was over the ridge she saw the river just in front of her down in the valley. It shone like a wide wavy ribbon in the dim light. She hurried down to the bank. Cold damp gusts from the foaming masses of water met her. How was she to get over? Nowhere could she see a bridge or a ford. The river roared and foamed, and it seemed to be laughing at the tiny human creature standing helplessly on the bank.

She ran alongside the river. In one place it narrowed, and here it was such a short distance to the other side that she might manage it if she took quick steps and ran over the big rocks standing up out of the foaming water. But she dared not venture out on to the slippery level rocks. Her courage failed her. Her body pained her with tiredness and cold.

Then she became aware of some shadows just below the steep crag of the mountain. It took a while before she realized they were horses. Frosty vapor rose from their bodies in the cold night air.

She staggered over to the horses. They stared at her with shiny eyes. The biggest of them, a strong black shaggy stallion, came trotting over to her.

Tir took hold of his mane and swung herself up on to the horse's back. Then she leaned her face against his soft, warm neck. She was so tired, so tired. It was good to lie like that and rest her painful legs while the horse sauntered off, calm and steady.

Then suddenly she felt the loud roar of the river in her ears, and felt the horse's gait grow unsteady and fumbling. She sat up with a jerk and saw foaming river water on both sides. So what she had prayed to St. Patrick had come true: the horse had found his way to the bridge over the river. That must be the way he went when he was taken down to the farm where it belonged. The bridge was so narrow the horse had difficulty walking along it. She could do nothing but close her eyes until she was across. She hung on to the mane and clung with her legs to the flanks as well as she could.

When she opened her eyes again she saw the river roaring wildly bubbling just behind them. They had done it! Good, kind horse! She sank down onto his back again and they went on over the lava plain. Images came and went before her eyes. As if in a fog she saw something dancing and moving about over below the mountains. The vapor moved over the ground and turned into strange figures in the cold moonlight.

Tir stared in horror. The earth steamed, it boiled and glowed. Suddenly boiling water gushed into the air as if from the nostrils of a snarling gigantic dragon. They would have to go past it. The black stallion carried her on confidently. He placed his hooves carefully and lightly among the boiling pools, and always trod on firm ground.

"Hurry along," whispered Tir. "I'm afraid I won't be able to hold on much longer."

She kicked the horse's sides and he set off at a trot over the level ground until they came to a ridge. There he stopped. Below them lay a whole settlement. The light of torches shone outside the house walls.

"Now you can go back, poor little horse," whispered Tir. "Thank you for carrying me over."

The farmstead she was heading for was the biggest in the settlement. It lay by itself high on a hilltop. The houses were low, with turf roofs and walls. The hot spring in the farmyard steamed.

The sound of singing and hoarse cries could be heard. Some women's voices cackled. Thin smoke rose towards the sky.

Tir crept closer. There was only one guard on watch. He lay with his shield over his stomach, asleep with open mouth. Tir tiptoed past the long side of the house. There she found a peephole and peered in.

To start with she saw only the light from rows of torches along the wall. But gradually she began to distinguish figures and faces. The men on the long bench were completely drunk. They raised the mead horn, bawled and sang. Some of them slumped over the table snoring loudly. Gissur sat in the high seat. He wasn't exactly an impressive sight. His face was red and shiny with sweat. He sang at the top of his voice and beat the table till the ale bowls ran over.

Tir ran her eyes over to the cross bench. Then she jumped. There sat Helga. She could hardly recognize her little playmate. She had a white linen kerchief on her

head, and wore a dress heavily ornamented on the chest. She too seemed to have tasted the mead, for she was fooling about, laughing and wagging her head. Tir didn't see how she could get hold of her. She stood there waiting for a long time, and in the end almost gave up hope. Then Helga suddenly stood up and walked unsteadily towards the door.

∼

Helga came from the lighted hall straight into the covered entry. It was pitch dark outside. She couldn't see a hand before her face. Then she heard whispering out there in the dark. Was it the wind, she wondered, and stayed quite still listening. It seemed like an icy breath wrapping around her shoulders. She pulled her cloak tightly around her and hurried back toward the door.

"Helga," came the whisper. "It's me, Tir!"

Then Helga stopped. She looked around fearfully. Slowly her eyes grew used to the dark. Her gaze passed along the turf wall. Right at the end by the corner post she glimpsed a small figure that was almost one with the night and the darkness. Only the face shone strangely white.

Helga had had a taste of the golden mead everyone celebrating in the hall was enjoying. She fumbled her way across the yard with unsteady steps, until she was right over by the post. "No, is it really you, Tir," she laughed a bit uncertainly. Her voice had a strange note. "How is it that you, a slave, come to visit a mighty housewife in this manner? If there's anything we don't like it's beggars loitering about among the farms here. I really ought to call one of my guards. Well, what do you want of me?"

Tir's eyes wavered like a frightened animal. "You've got to help me, Helga," she whispered. "Do you hear, Helga—

you must help me!"

Helga felt the mead fizzing in her head. She chuckled. "Follow me then," she said.

Tir went with Helga and kept close to her. Helga's big cloak almost completely hid her. Just at the end of the covered way they came upon a man carrying a big over-flowing bowl of mead. He bawled and sang and nodded to his mistress as she walked past. But further along the passage he turned and scratched his gray tufts of hair in bewilderment. "By Odin," he mumbled. "I'm sure I saw the mistress had four legs! The mead must be really strong tonight."

Helga took hold of one of the candleholders placed in the wall and climbed up a steep flight of steps. The light flickered over a door covered with woodcarvings and iron fittings. "This is where I sleep." She took a little bronze key from her belt and unlocked the door. "This is not a place for slaves," she said. "But you'd better come in, since you've got something important to tell me."

She went into the room first and Tir went fumbling after her. They were in a room as big as the living room at Brede's house. Helga bustled around lighting the candles along the walls, so it was almost as light as day. Along one wall was a bed with carved horses' heads, and the bed had pillows filled with down. "Feel," said Helga. "Have you ever had anything so nice and soft in your hands. And look here." Helga ran over to a chest with golden fittings. She opened it and spread the contents on the floor. Surely no one had ever seen such fine clothes! The light shone on bright silks and beautiful woven bands, on furs and embroidery. The finest dress was a red shift with golden decorations on the bodice. "Do you want to see my trea-sure chest too?" Helga brought out a small casket she kept in a ledge on the wall. She emptied out the contents.

Beautiful pearls glittered, mountain crystal and blue-colored glass, and golden amber, shone. Helga let the pearls run through her fingers, smiling proudly.

"I am the mistress of this farm now," she said, moving into the light. She knew she was looking good. A whole bunch of keys hung from the belt round her waist; one to her room, one to the hall, one to the barn, and lots of little keys to caskets and chests around the farmstead. The keys rattled and jangled as she walked to and fro.

Tir sank down on one of the benches in the room. She was so cold she shook all over. Her head began to sink on to her chest while she stared at Helga whirling to and fro before her. A red streak ran from the wound in her arm.

Then Helga suddenly stopped in the middle of the floor and fixed her eyes on Tir. It was as if her head suddenly cleared. "Tir," she called, and fell on her knees before her. "But you're wounded, Tir! By Freya, I think you're going to faint, girl!"

As in a dream Tir glimpsed Helga opening the heavy door and calling one of her slaves. "Fetch me hot water," she cried. A steaming tub appeared in a moment. Helga wrenched off her party clothes. She got out some rags, which she dipped in water and started to bathe Tir's arm. "Don't scream," she said sternly, "or they'll hear us and come rushing up the stairs." Tir gritted her teeth, but the tears ran down her cheeks while Helga bandaged the wound.

"How can this have happened," mumbled Helga, helping Tir off with her clothes.

"I did try to explain," Tir whispered. Her words came in fits and starts, and incoherently.

But this time Helga listened.

"Creep into my bed," said Helga. "And lie close to the wall. Starkodd is dead drunk with his head in his bowl. No one will come up here tonight."

Tir sank down into the soft quilts. Her body was heavy and drowsy, and her wounded arm burned like fire. Confused, flickering images flashed behind her closed eyes: riders rushing out of the dark with flashing swords, Reim being seized and taken prisoner, the foaming river water, and the plain with the fog beings dancing under the mountain.

~

Next day word went round that the mistress of the house was out of sorts. She kept her sleeping room and wanted food and water sent up. No one thought that was strange. The day after a ritual celebration it wasn't only the mistress whose legs wouldn't bear her. The master himself had rolled under the long table in the hall and lay in a snoring sleep with his head in a pool of dirty ale and fatty scraps of food. The maidservants had chucked a sheepskin over him, and one of them had fallen for the temptation to empty the rest of the mead bowl over his swollen face. Now it looked as if he lay swimming in pork and mead.

"Eat this," said Helga, holding out some pieces of meat to Tir. "Here's some sour milk for you to drink with it."

"I haven't the strength. I'm so tired."

Tir sank back on the pillows. Her body would not obey her. The wound in her arm hurt all the time.

Helga ate some of the meat. Then she started to tidy up the dresses and jewelry and pearls scattered over the floor. She flung it into the big chest in the corner. Suddenly the tears came. Her shoulders shook and trembled. "What do I want with all these things!" She trampled on the red silk shift and kicked at some of the jewels on the floor. "I'm sick with longing for Mother and Father and all my sisters

130 and brothers. And the twin sisters of mine I wanted to bring with me. Every time I sit on the high seat with Starkodd I wish I were in our lovely place in the forest, where we played with bows and arrows. Can you remember that?"

Yes, of course Tir remembered it. She nodded weakly.

"Running barefoot out there in the fields was better than wearing soft calfskin shoes in the hall here," whispered Helga. She sniffed and wept. Her face was just as freckled and childish as before beneath the housewife's kerchief. "There will be an heir here on this farm in the autumn. That's what everybody has been waiting for, no doubt."

Then she rose and dried her nose with the back of her hand. "Now we must see what we're going to do with you." She began to walk up and down. "One thing is certain anyway. You can't stay here. Starkodd is Narve's uncle. You couldn't come closer to the viper's nest than you have now."

She opened the door and whispered out into the darkness: "Drumba, are you there?" A gray shadow appeared in the doorway.

"I know your legs are bad, Drumba, but I hope you can go off with the message I'm going to give you now. You're the only one I can trust here."

Drumba quickly understood what Helga wanted. She slipped across the farmyard and soon vanished into the shadows.

Tir sank into a deep heavy sleep. She lay like that all day until the light faded. Then she vaguely felt herself being lifted up in a safe embrace and carried away, across the yard of Starkodd's farmstead and out into the night.

～

Digralde walked restlessly to and fro in his house. "I must go east," he said curtly. "A slave's life isn't worth much when the big eagles get their claws in."

Una stood before him. "This isn't wise of you, Digralde. The chieftain has plenty of men, and they have sharp weapons."

"I can't rest," Digralde growled. "I know now what happened to Reim. I met that little slave boy with the black mop, Amed, below the mountain yesterday, and he told me what happened. If they don't put an end to Reim they'll probably try to get him back to Norway where the earl's family live." Digralde seized his broad-edged farmer's axe, and hung a pair of big smith's tongs from his belt. He stopped at the threshold. "There's a ship sailing from the bay in just a few days. It's going right over to the Irish Sea..."

Una stared at him with big eyes: "But that ship belongs to Ossur, Narve's father..."

"Not everything is as easy as downing a good cut of pork," said Digralde. "Three days after Narve is buried Ossur and his men will ride west with the goods for the ship's cargo. It's my hope that Bentein can help us. He has goods to sell in Ireland. But if we are to get the youngsters on board the ship..."

Una listened, all ears.

Digralde went on: "If we're to get them on board, it must be done with cunning. Do you remember the little mountain cave where Astrid played last summer?"

Una's eyes turned to the sleeping bench. Tir's face was white beneath the coppery hair. She lay with mouth half open. Her eyes were closed.

The bad arm lay outside the sheepskin like a withered flower.

"Yes, all right," nodded Una. "I'll show her the place. May Tor and Freya and all the gods protect you, Digralde."

Digralde fetched his horse, harnessed it and swung into the saddle. Then he rode without stopping until he reached Bredesgard. There he asked Brede if he could help him to get a bearskin from the time he was a bear hunter.

~

Tir was inside a thick red fog. The smell of nauseating herbs, of steam and fire, disturbed her. She tried to get up but couldn't. She wanted to scream, but the sound stopped somewhere down in her throat. She seemed to be floating round in a pot of bubbling witches' brew, while the troll hags moved around grimacing horribly in front of her. The witch's brew scalded her skin and pulled her down into still hotter depths that boiled and seethed. "Help me," she panted. "Help me!" She lay there a long time struggling and sweating.

Then she seemed able to get hold of the edge of the pot. At last she managed to raise herself. At the same moment the troll hags whirled away, and the glowing heat lessened its hold on her body. She went on lying there in a daze. She heard voices rising and falling. She glimpsed figures coming close and disappearing again, like shadows in the dusk. Slowly the red fog went away. And suddenly she seemed to be walking into a forest—a great light forest where the sunrays filtered down through the trees. She lifted up her face. There it was again! The blue bird! It hovered high above the treetops, and moved so silently it seemed to be sailing in the air. The bird lowered its head down among the transparent leaves. It turned into a human face. A well known reassuring face. Tir struggled to collect her thoughts. Then the features grew clearer. "Is it you, Una...I must have been asleep a long time..."

"That's true enough," smiled Una. "You've been lying here unconscious for seven whole days. That was a nasty wound you got in your arm, my girl. But Una knows how to make use of herbs and magic arts to trick the goddesses of fate."

She brought a bundle of sheepskins. "Wait a moment, I'll lift you up so you can see where you are, at least. Digralde is farmer on this place now, after his father died last winter."

Tir looked around her. It wasn't a big room. It was built of strong driftwood and turf, but she found it hard to believe Digralde could manage to stand upright under the low ceiling. It was nice and warm in there, even though the wind whistled around the corners of the house.

Then she heard whispering outside. "Hush," someone said. "Remember Tir is ill. We must be as quiet as mice so we don't wake her."

"Here's someone who opened her eyes long ago!" Una went over to open the door. Tir felt happiness leap in her heart. There they all were—the people she had known when she was a slave of the earl in Norway. There was Sigrid and all her little sons. And there was Tora she had played with while she herded the cows. Tora held a wriggling two-year-old in her arms. A strong little girl smiling all over her face and showing off her baby teeth. She pulled Tora's long braids and pretended they were a horse's reins. "Gee up, go on, old dobbin," she crowed, chortling with fun.

"Astrid robber-girl," scolded Tora, shaking the child.

"You guessed right if you think this is my little daughter," said Una. "She's the one the earl would have left out for the wolves because she was a slave girl. Now she's bigger and stronger than many a boy child of the same age." Una laughed. "Yes, she gets mad at them if they tease her, and she isn't afraid of anything on earth. And here is the new little one," said Una, holding out a fiery red little bundle. "She's not so bad, either, Astrid's little sister!"

Tora went over to the sleeping bench where Tir lay. She stood there, feeling a bit shy. Everything seemed to have changed between them. The bridge of Tora's nose had grown narrower, and her freckles were gone. But she had the same merry blue spark in her eyes.

"This flower is for you," she said. "It's the first one I've found this year. I think it suits you. It's as hard to kill as you are. Pushing its head up through clay and gravel, even after a hard winter."

Tir stroked the tousled yellow bud. She seemed to be waking up out of a long trance. Suddenly she remembered everything that had happened. She threw aside blankets and fleece and tried to stand on her feet.

"What's happened to Reim," she almost screamed out. "He might be dead already."

Una wrinkled her brows and pushed her back on to the bench. "You must be thankful you have saved your own life," she said severely. "Tonight I'm going out to kill a sheep. The sacrificial fire will burn and the magic words will rise up to Valhalla. Everything will turn out for the best for Reim and Digralde."

~

"I've come to say goodbye to you," said Helga. "Here's a piece of the rye cake you like so much."

"You look happy!"

"I've been to see an old soothsayer who can see into the future," said Helga. "She foretold Starkodd's death."

Tir stared at her, horrified.

"He has had luck with him through twenty years of Viking raiding," said Helga. "But the prophecy says it's the mead that will be the end of him eventually. It will come to just about the same thing whether he sits in his hall and pours mead down his throat, or carouses with other Vikings in Valhalla."

Tir couldn't help laughing.

"Don't you realize," whispered Helga, "that if I'm left alone on the farmstead, I shall be the one who decides things. My little one will inherit the place, but I shall manage the whole estate all the time until the heir is full grown and of legal age. And then perhaps I'll be able to marry someone I like."

"I wonder who that would be," Tir wondered.

Helga smiled shyly. "There's someone I care a lot about," she said. "If I get him I shall be happy. He was daft enough to go out with the Vikings, and then he lost an arm, but I'm sure he can hold me tight enough with the other one."

Tir smiled. It wasn't hard to guess who Helga meant.

Helga pressed something into Tir's hand. "Take this," she said. "The merchant must have some silver for taking you over the sea."

Tir embraced everyone in the little room. Then she and Una set out on the road that led down to the shore. The moon had not yet risen over the mountain, and no one saw them go.

Chapter Three

Tir jumped. The dry branches on the forest floor crackled again. This time the sound was closer. She was sure someone was approaching with cautious steps.

If only she could be free of the horrible fear, thought Tir. She had been sitting here waiting in this cramped cave ever since midnight. The moon had risen over the ridge now. The sea shone like a gigantic bowl of silver, only the high cliffs to the northwest threw shadows over the surface. This was where the ship had been wrecked during the stormy night more than a year ago. The sea washed and washed over the dead men down there in the depths.

Then she heard a faint whistle. It sounded rather like a seabird calling far off. She felt warmth spread through her whole body. Now Reim was coming. Now he was coming at last.

Just then she saw them come running down the path. In the clear moonlight she could clearly see Digralde with his *bearskin round his shoulders and Reim in his brown sheepskin jacket. The man carrying a big sack must be the Irish merchant. But she was surprised to see that the little black-haired boy from the chieftain's farmstead was with the others.*

The Irish merchant greeted her in his mother tongue: "You must have been beside yourself with terror, my girl," he said, helping her from the cave.

"Poof," said Tir, "but it was a long time to wait."

Digralde chuckled. "I've never had a harder job than it was to get Bentein to tear himself away from his sweetheart here in Iceland."

Digralde opened his arms wide and the three children were lost in his embrace. "Not long now till we set off," he said. His voice was strangely muffled. "Before sunrise Ossur Svarte will bring the goods to be embarked. It'll be best if you stay hidden if you want to stay alive."

He seemed to want to say more, for he stood for a while tugging Reim's forelock with his huge hand.

Then he turned and walked off into the dark forest.

~

"Hide yourselves here inside the tent," said Bentein.

They made themselves small and crept in together behind the stack of skins furthest back in the corner. They lay there still as mice listening to the sound of the sea lapping against the ship's side. Tir was so tired after the long night's watch that she fell asleep with her head on a soft sheepskin. But just afterward she was woken by a clattering inside the tent and a deep voice saying: "Put the goods here, men. Stow the things well. There's a lot to get in."

Reim started to tremble when he heard Ossur Svarte's voice. "Lie still," said Tir. She clutched Reim so tightly that her nails pierced his palms. Ossur and his men

138

crashed around for a long time. They rolled barrels into place and stowed heavy chests and sacks. The cargo was made up of all kinds of goods, homespun and feathers, walrus bones, wool and train oil, goatskins and brimstone.

"Have a good look around for any runaways," said Ossur. "I'm plagued by bad luck. Two wretches of slaves disappeared from my place last night, an Irish redhead and a dark-skinned lad from Arabia. My people say evil powers were about, but I think this business has a natural explanation."

Bentein managed a short laugh. "I assure you, Ossur, the only living things on board this ship are the fleas hiding in this pile of skins!"

Ossur laughed and punched the skins with the flat of

his hand. "Yes, it would be a strange day when runaway slaves escape from the frying pan only to make straight for the fire!" He gave Bentein his hand. "There's a fair wind blowing. Promise me you'll make a good deal and look out for pirates on the voyage!"

"If all goes well we'll be back before the winter storms set in," said Bentein.

~

The ship glided away from the shore. Tir felt Amed's hand take hers. He seemed to want to feel whether it was really true.

Not until the ship was well out to sea did they dare come out. They kept close to Bentein the whole time.

A white-bearded man stood in the prow arranging ropes. "We should have left earlier," he grumbled. "The wind was fairer yesterday. But it's important for several ships to stay together in the waters we're making for. There's no shortage of Vikings and robbers!"

Then he caught sight of the three children hiding behind Bentein's back, and his eyes darkened still more. "What kind of crew is that you've got there, may I ask? Are we to have suckling kids too, that only eat from the sack and don't know the right end of an oar! I don't even need to ask if you're trying to get runaway slaves away. I know you, Bentein. You're a good merchant, but soft as butter when it comes to women and slave kids!"

"If I know you, Havtor, this will soften you," Bentein said while slipping him some coins. "This ought to be enough for you to keep your mouth shut!"

Havtor grabbed the silver with a greedy fist. He smiled toothlessly and went on stretching ropes. Tir didn't hear him ask again where they came from or where they were going.

Tir and Reim stood by the ship's rail. They made their farewells to Iceland with their eyes. Over there, thought Tir, in the shadow of the sacred mountain, hidden beneath moss and turf, lies a rune stick engraved with magical words. She would never know whether it was the power of the runes or all the prayers she had sent to the saints in heaven that had brought them to where they were now.

She recalled the faces of Bergliot and Brede. She was ashamed to have left Bredesgard without a word. She knew she would feel the pain of that as long as she lived.

Then there was Helga—little, childish Helga, her playmate at Ingolfsgard—who had defied her mighty clan to help some poor slaves. Tir thought she would always be able to bring to mind the round blue eyes and freckled nose when she thought of Helga, even if she lived to be a hundred.

But the worst thing had been to leave Una and Digralde. They had been firm friends ever since she and her brother were seized by the Vikings and taken to the earl's farmstead in Norway. Never had she met such strong and brave people as they were. They would stay in her mind with other good memories she had stored up forever.

She felt like forgetting all the bad things she had experienced, as the sea washed and flushed over seaweed and rocks hidden down in the depths.

Tir let her arm slide along the rail. As if by chance she opened her hand and dropped what she had been holding. The little bundle vanished in the white waves foaming around the bow. In it was the small knife, the steel and the bone spoon she had used while she was a slave. The bundle sank down into the depths and was gone.

When she looked up again Iceland had disappeared in

the morning mist. There was nothing but blue sea and sky around them on all sides.

"What happened, Reim," she asked. "What happened after Ossur Svarte's people took you prisoner?"

"It's a long story," said Reim. "There are many things I'd rather forget..."

But all the same she gradually came to know what had happened.

～

After the warriors had seized Reim they took him to their chieftain.

Reim was frantic with terror when he was brought into the great hall. It was dark in there. A few flaming torches threw light over the walls. Behind the gray smoke from the fire he could make out faces. Sword hilts and axes flashed.

They were many. He was alone.

They were grown fighting men. He was barely twelve winters old, and he was a slave.

Reim felt his heart hammering. It beat in his chest, his forehead, the palms of his hands. He felt his heartbeats filled the whole room. Now they can hear it, he thought. They can hear how frightened I am.

In the center of the long bench, between the grinning heads of the posts of the high seat, sat Ossur Svarte. He got slowly to his feet and walked across the floor. The men made way. The gold jewels on his broad chest glittered. A sword half hidden beneath his wide cloak flashed. He went close up to Reim. Reim felt his breath straight in his face. "You, most miserable of any creature crawling around on earth," he snarled. "You have killed the best future chieftain in Iceland."

"Kill him at once, Father," came a young man's voice.

The chieftain's lips were narrow. Reim could hardly hear the words he uttered:

"My warriors could have made away with you at once. But I shall wait. I shall allow myself the pleasure of watching you die."

Reim felt like screaming. His mouth opened, but not a sound came from his throat. Terror spread like red fog before his eyes. He jerked his body about like a cornered animal trying to flee.

The warriors were on him like a shot. They seized him and held him tight. At a quick sign from the chieftain they wrenched off his jacket. He stood there with his naked back before the line of men. He hunched up his shoulders as if trying to hide his head between his shoulder blades.

The chieftain stretched out his hands. He held a whip.

Reim struggled with himself. Once before, while he was in Norway, he had felt the whiplash on his back. It was when he had lost a flock of sheep belonging to the great earl. Then he had been beaten until his back was like glowing fire.

When he saw the whip in the chieftain's hands he could not keep himself upright any longer. He fell down at the feet of the warriors. He clawed at the floor as if he wanted to hide under its earth.

But each time the whip came whistling down he tensed his body and tried to get to his feet.

~

When he opened his eyes he couldn't see a hand before his face. The room he was in was as dark as the night itself. He didn't know how long he had been lying there, but it must have been for days. He lay there in a stupor. He wept. Terror and loneliness had overpowered him. He was naked and cold, but his skinless back burned like fire. He had not the strength to sit up but lay stretched out on the bare earthen floor. There was nothing in the room but a couple of stiff sheepskins. But they didn't give much warmth.

When he sank down into sleep he forgot everything for a while. But then the nightmares came. He lay on a heap of glowing coals burning into his skin. The pain surged through his body.

Then he woke up and knew the reality was even worse. He fervently wished he was dead. He wept bitterly because St. Patrick would not hear his prayers.

The thought of death had come to him a few times before. Some of his friends of the same age had passed away when the plague raged in his home village in Ireland. Sometimes even newborn children died. His mother had talked a lot about the little brother who only lived for a few days.

But the possibility of his own death had never occurred to him before. Not even when he and Tir had been captured by the Vikings did he think of it. He had felt disheartened then. Disheartened and frightened. But he had clung to hope like a shipwrecked person to a floating mast.

Now he knew he was going to die. Even the heavenly powers could not help him.

When the pain overwhelmed him vague pictures flickered through his head. He could see his home village and the little farm with black and white cattle grazing. He saw the dark green fields and the great oak forest with its light and shadow. He saw the small monastery church with ivy climbing up the gray stone walls.

He wept and dug his nails into the hard-trodden earth floor. He was twelve years old and was going to die.

He felt he had only just started out on life.

Then he raised his head and listened. Sounds from the world outside reached him. He heard noise and din and horses neighing. Ossur's relatives must have arrived for the funeral of the chieftain's son.

Reim realized that the cellar he was imprisoned in was directly beneath the chieftain's hall, for there was tramping and noise just over his head. They began to chant up there. They sang and murmured all night long. There was one song about Odin, the god of death, and life in Valhalla, the dwelling of the gods. There went all of those killed by weapons, and there battle and war would go on through all eternity.

Reim gave a start. He was quite sure he heard a voice close by. There was someone outside the door.

"Reim," came a whisper. "It's me, Amed!"

Reim felt joy like a small warm flame in his body. He was not quite alone with the fear and the darkness after all.

Amed struggled with the Norse language. "Here, some bread for you. It's my turn this time."

Reim fumbled across the floor and found the bread. There was a small opening at the bottom of the door, maybe from when a mouse had gnawed a hole in it.

"Thanks," whispered Reim.

"Door bolted with iron lock," stammered Amed. "Or we run away together. Now I must go."

Reim listened to the steps creeping away. Then he was alone again.

He chewed at the crust, trying to make it last as long as possible. Gradually silence fell on the chieftain's hall. He guessed most of the guests had fallen asleep over their mead.

The day after the funeral a small company rode up to Ossur Svarte's farmstead. A young woman, almost a girl, sat upon the leading horse, wrapped in a gray hooded cloak. Outside the entrance to the hall she pushed back her hood and jumped down from her horse. Her eyes shone with determination. She signed to her men to wait outside. They tethered the horses to a post and lined up, resting on their spears. They stood there unmoving as the small girlish figure walked toward the chieftain's house. From inside she could hear the women mourners singing. They sounded like wolves howling at the moon. Just below the mountain crag to the north lay a newly built burial mound.

The chieftain, Ossur Svarte, came out into the yard. His wife walked just behind him, a small pale woman with her face half hidden in her linen kerchief.

"And what errand do you come on, kinswoman, that you cannot send one of your slaves with?"

"A slave cannot carry out every errand properly," said Helga. She struggled to speak as adult, sober-minded women did. "If it surprises you not to see Starkodd, it is because he is sitting over his mead and is not very capable of speaking. And still less could he manage to sit astride a horse!" She looked at them disapprovingly and said: "Strange customs rule in this house, when someone who has ridden all night is not invited in to house and hospitality."

Ossur made way for Helga to enter the hall. He sighed: "It is sorrow that makes me bitter, dear kinswoman. He who loses his son cannot be other than sorrowful."

"You are not so sorrowful that you do not think of revenge," said Helga, placing herself before Ossur. She was not tall enough to reach higher than his chest. She put her hands on her hips and threw back her head: "You have a slave in your custody who belongs, as far as I understand, to the farmer called Brede. I request you to release this slave as quickly as possible."

Ossur stared at Helga in disbelief. Then he knitted his brow and roared: "You must be out of your mind, kinswoman. Have you come all this way to beg for the life of a slave! I can tell you at once that was a long journey for nothing."

"It's Brede I am asking for," said Helga. "Brede is an honorable man who still has not a single enemy in the settlement."

Ossur struck the ridgepole with his fist. "The slave must die," he yelled. "And besides, I know for certain that the slave belongs to the earl back in Norway. If this small farmer Brede demands the slave back, I shall surely see to it there is not much left of the farmstead he has toiled to build here."

Now Helga's eyes flamed up. She waved her fist just under Ossur's nose. "That sounds like a man who is great in body but paltry as the smallest worm in mind," she shrieked. "How can you be so sure it was the slave who committed this crime?"

Ossur too had gone white in the face. He dug his hand into a ledge in the wall and flung a used arrow on the table. "If you can read runes," he grunted, "perhaps you can read the name for yourself."

"It is Reim's arrow," nodded Helga.

Ossur chuckled. "You couldn't have better evidence than that of the murderer's identity," he said curtly. Now, dear kinswoman, you can go home again with your company."

"I will not leave till I've said this," thundered Helga:

"There are three of us free people in this settlement, all over fifteen winters old, who are willing to witness at the Ting in this case. Reim had a good bow that seldom missed whatever it was aimed at. It is true that the arrows were marked with Reim's name. But it is also true that Grim Gussursson stole the bow from Reim when we were once out having a shooting competition in the meadow."

Ossur leaned forward in the high seat and searched her face. "Is this true, what you are saying, kinswoman?"

"You'll find the witnesses at Snorresgard and Toresgard," said Helga. "That's where our friends we played with that day live. If you like, you can go and see them. But I'm afraid you'll get the same answer there…"

Ossur grew thoughtful. His eyes turned into cold black stones. "So it was Grim then, the son of Gissur Lodinsson," he mumbled slowly. "There's never been real peace between our clans…"

He stood up and tightened his belt. "Get out your sharp weapons," he shouted to the men at the long table below. "Find the best swords and spears. We shall have a use for them today!"

His wife Tjodhild had been sitting at the end of the table listening to all that was said. Now she rose. She was fragile as a sparrow, but she had authority all the same, standing there with her housewife's kerchief around her head and all the keys of the farmstead at her belt.

"It would be better to bring up your sons in other ways, Ossur," she said, "than with thoughts of revenge. It was a hard loss to have Narve torn from us, but all the same, don't let this lead to more misdeeds. One day there must be peace between our clans. Our son was not entirely without guilt either, he could be so ready for a fight and so proud…"

Ossur pushed her aside. "Put on your armor, men," he

ordered. "We have more important things afoot than messing about with women."

"But what about Reim," said Helga. "Brede's slave..."

Ossur pulled his coat of mail over his head and fastened his sword firmly in his belt. "I'm sick of all this chatter," he roared. "The slave brat can be happy he's allowed to stay alive. Greet Brede from me and say that if he bought the slave legally at market, I shall make good the silver he demands. But as soon as I come back I'll have the slave sent back to Norway. Perhaps that'll teach other slaves it doesn't really pay to run away from their master..."

It was evening at Bredesgard.

"I think I can hear the clatter of weapons," said Bergliot, looking out of the peep hole. She put her hand to her mouth when she saw the great file of armed men riding horses with flowing manes. "Now they're coming, Brede," she whispered. "May all the gods of Valhalla protect us." Their sons gripped their weapons. Ravn held his spear in his good hand.

Brede's face shone white in the dull light filtering in through the smoke hole. "If only they don't burn down the farmstead," he said quietly. "It's cost me so much toil to build it up."

They sat waiting in breathless suspense.

Then Bergliot cried out again: "Well, I never...they're riding past the farm!"

"You must be seeing things," said Brede. "Which way are they going?"

"Westward," said Bergliot excitedly. "Toward Gissur's place."

"Then they must have found the right murderer, I think," said Brede. "Now there's a new feud brewing among the chieftains' clans."

Brede and Bergliot looked tensely to the west along the valley. But they didn't see any smoke coming from there and heard nothing to indicate a fight.

Later on they heard the reason.

Aud was at Gissur's farmstead that day. Gissur had sent for her because he had discovered something new about the fire on his farm. When she saw the warriors coming she went out into the yard and stood in front of the line of men.

"Get out of the way, now, Aud," called Ossur Svarte.

"First I wish to hear what brings you here," said Aud.

"I am not coming on a peaceful errand," screamed Ossur. "Anyone who doesn't know my son was buried yesterday must be blind and deaf. I know now that the killer isn't any scoundrel of a slave but a chieftain's son." He held up the broken arrow. "Now we're here in force to fetch the bow this arrow belongs to. I am not far wrong if I say it's here."

Then Grim came to the door, supported by his brother and father. He was as white as a ghost and his eyes were like two dark holes. His father spoke:

"Here is the bow," he called, throwing it on the ground in front of Ossur. "It has brought nothing but bane with it. My son has kept a reminder of his fight with Narve: a wound that almost severed his leg. He has been unconscious since that night of misdeeds, and he'll never be a promising chieftain again. If the arrow hadn't struck Narve it might have been my son who had ended up in Valhalla."

"He'll get there anyway," snarled Ossur, drawing his sword. "But mark this, it was not our clan who broke the peace!"

Then Aud ran in front of his horse. Her skirt and

kerchief blew almost straight out in the strong wind. "That's what I call breaking the peace," she shouted— "burning down the farms in this settlement!"

"Watch what you say, Aud!" Ossur's eyes darkened. "What you mean is that it was someone from my farm who was guilty of setting fire to Gissur's farmstead!"

"This was found just by the burned timbers," said Aud, holding out her hand. "It is a silver pin I know your family has owned for many generations." Ossur bent down. He picked up the pin and stared at it for a long time. Those nearest him said afterward they saw something wet shine in the eyes of the stout chieftain.

"The pin belonged to Narve," he said quietly. "It was given to him as firstborn son when he took his first steps on the farmstead back in Norway."

He pushed his sword back into the scabbard. For a long time he sat silent on his horse: "I'm in no mood for fighting now I've seen this little bit of silver," he said at last. "Aud the Wise is right. We'd better ride back to our farmstead."

But back at Ossur's farm everything was in an uproar. Slaves and servants ran around like scared hens. While the chieftain and his men were away a huge male bear had come into the farmyard. It marched with a rolling gait on its hind legs over to the prison room, broke the lock and carried off the Irish slave. No one had ever seen anything like it. Horror took over the farm. The powers of darkness must be abroad. And the strange thing was that the black-haired slave from Arabia had vanished too.

At Bredesgard Bergliot was raking over the ashes on the hearth for the night. "There've been many strange things happening tonight," she said, "that will be talked about for many years in this settlement."

She went to sit on the long bench beside her husband and sons. She slid her hand into Brede's great fist. "I thank the goddesses of destiny that peace has come to us," she said quietly. "And yet I feel worried. I can't help thinking of two Irish children far out at sea on the way to their homeland."

The ship made straight for the Hebrides. Havtor had goods to unload there and fresh cargo to take on board. The little Arab boy wanted to get off the ship there. He knew some people there, he said. When he was captured and taken north from his homeland, the Viking ships had moored for a while in a Hebridean harbor. Amed had been ill then; he had an attack of plague that burned and tormented him. The Vikings had taken him to a kind young woman who was a healer. If only he could find her home it might be a way later on of finding a ship bound for his homeland.

Tir and Reim were thoughtful as they watched him go. It was a long way to Arabia. It lay right at the far side of the big world. None of them believed Amed would ever get there. But they could not bring themselves to disappoint him. His dark eyes shone like stars when his feet were firmly planted on the earth of the Hebrides, islands with poor land in the middle of the great windblown ocean. "Farewell," they called, and the boy replied in his own tongue.

They sailed by the sun by day and the stars by night.

Only once did they have poor visibility. But that was at such a convenient time that Bentein wondered whether St. Patrick himself was holding a protective hand over them. It happened when they were midway between the

Hebrides and the Irish Sea. Then they suddenly caught sight of a ship some way off. The ships made good speed in the fresh breeze. The big square sails were filled with wind.

During the time they had been at sea they had seen many ships, but always a long way off. This ship was making straight for them.

"The people on board probably need help of some kind," Reim thought. "Perhaps they've run out of fresh water..."

Havtor laughed grimly. "No, these fellows aren't likely to be after fresh water." He bit his lips. "I recognize the figureheads and the marks on the sail. They are Vikings and pirates!"

Now everyone on board grew uneasy. "People like that don't wait till they get ashore to plunder," growled Bentein. "It's a fool that doesn't know there's good trade in robbing a ship full of goods. Now, men, we must make use of everything we've learned of seamanship!"

Everyone put their trust in old Havtor. He had sailed between Norway and Iceland and the western islands for a whole lifetime. He always said of himself that what he didn't know about ships and sailing wasn't worth knowing. If anyone tried giving advice he'd turn into an angry lemming. "Landlubbers," he screamed and scolded them, "seasick farmers!"

In his time as a sailing merchant Havtor had been pursued by Vikings almost every summer, but had always managed to escape.

Now he stood at the helm and sang out one order after another to the crew. The ship ploughed through the waves so the spray covered the decks. The sail billowed like a tight bow from the mast.

But the Viking ships were catching up. They were so

close they could see the men on board. Behind the shields hanging along the rail helmeted heads and shining weapons appeared. Soon they would be within range.

Then suddenly the sun grew dark. A mist rolled over the surface of the sea and soon the ship was enveloped in gray fog as thick as the wool on a sheep. They sailed at random, unable to see a hand before their faces. When the fog lifted, the dragon ship with the armed Vikings had gone.

Tir's back was freezing. Whether good or evil powers had been with them she had felt a cold gust down her neck. It was as if the sea specter itself had reared its head out of the sea and breathed fog and mist around the ships. But Havtor laughed happily, and said he would bet his beard on this brisk sail shortening their voyage by several days.

~

Tir knew that even if she lived to be a hundred she would never forget the day they sailed into Dublin. It was like waking up after a long, long night to a golden morning with sun glittering in the air and on the water. And in this wonderful light the town rose up before her, with its small and great houses, with battlements and towers. The ship danced on top of the waves. She stood right up in the bows and felt joy trickling through her body from her head right down to her toes. She was like a bewitched princess returning to her homeland after many years of imprisonment. The ship was the bird of freedom carrying her off on its strong wings straight to the green isle she knew so well. The air rushed and swelled with the sounds of the numerous bells, and there stood the people of Ireland waiting...

"Patrick," she called, throwing her arms round his

neck. "I'm so happy I must hug you. We've come home to Ireland!"

"That's nothing to make such a fuss about!" Patrick tore himself free of her embrace and turned away. Then she saw his eyes were brimming with tears. His shoulders shook. He sniffed and dried his face with the back of his hand.

Had they believed in earnest they would ever get back home? All the time they were slaves in Norway they had hardly dared to talk about their mother, father and Grandmother Gaelion and their little brothers and sisters. They had carried the thoughts of them inside and kept all the good memories like precious treasure. Only now did they realize they were free. Everything was like a lovely dream. They were back in the country where they belonged. They'd come back to the secret forests, the luxuriant Irish fields full of wild flowers and grasses, and the wide blue sky arching over St. Patrick's green isle.

"Ready with the hawser!" Havtor's thundering voice rang over the deck. They steered for one of the big wharfs of the town, and then the crew had their hands full making the ship secure. There was a general noise on board. On the wharf men ran to and fro pointing and waving to show where the ship was to lie. Reim had to jump ashore with the mooring rope.

"I guess you can breathe more freely now," said Bentein. He punched Reim in the side. "Take care to keep well away from Vikings and pirates in the future."

Bentein needed help with unloading all the goods, so now Tir and Reim had to toil at carrying leather sacks and barrels ashore. A stout man stood on the wharf taking charge of each load Bentein threw down to him. "What have you got in those sacks," laughed the fellow. "They're as big as houses but weigh less than the air we breathe."

"Birds' feathers from Iceland," Bentein shouted back. "And here's yard upon yard of homespun—catch! And look here!" Bentein jumped ashore and untied the rope around one of the sacks. "Just look here, here's a bit of everything to tempt the Dublin girls with!" He pulled out a white fox fur that shone like snow in the bright morning light. The fat man stroked the fur with the back of his hand and nodded appreciation. He could probably get any price he asked for such fine furs.

Bentein and the merchant loaded all the goods on to a cart and pulled it over the wharves toward one of the harbor booths. Tir and Reim strolled after them. Ships were packed alongside the wharves side by side, and everywhere merchants were unloading and loading their ships. Tir thought she had never seen so much life and movement. And that there were so many people in the world as these gathered together in Dublin, she couldn't begin to understand. She looked down the narrow alleyways that led from the harbor shops in toward the town. They were swarming with children playing and scrabbling around, women carrying boxes and buckets, men pulling small carts with goods or carrying big loads on their backs. The best-dressed of them didn't carry anything at all. She saw men in fur-lined cloaks with silver-ornamented belts and golden swords. Then she stood and gaped in wonderment at some girls walking in a group along the street. They looked about the same age as she was. They wore long dresses that seemed to be made of the finest silk, the material shone and glittered so as they walked. The bodices were covered with gold jewelry and precious stones. They moved with straight backs looking neither to the right or the left.

"Come on," called Reim, "what are you dawdling about for?"

She trotted after the others. On both sides of the street were houses woven of brushwood and caulked with clay. Smoke drifted into the air from the smoke holes and lay like gray fog over all the roofs of the town. People went in and out the doors the whole time. In one place a man was driving his goats into an enclosure just behind his house, the goats held back, and the man cursed and swore. In another place there was a well where some small girls hauled and pulled ropes on buckets they were filling with water. In a third place some children were playing a ring game in the middle of the street, so Bentein had to scold them to get them out of the way. There were so many houses Tir was afraid of getting lost and not finding the way back. It was best to keep close to the others.

They stopped in front of a big house in the middle of the town. At the same moment the door opened and a tall man came toward Bentein with open arms. "So the sea hasn't got the better of you yet," he said, laughing so the sound rang across the street. "You've kept the knack of using your sea legs, you old sea eagle!"

Reim and Tir were startled. They stood still, petrified. The man spoke Norwegian. Now they heard children running around speaking the Norse tongue too. They couldn't understand it. For they were in Dublin. They were back in Ireland, yet everyone around them spoke the Norwegian language. An icy fear crept down Tir's back.

"Come along," called Bentein, telling Tir and Reim to hurry up and help him get all the sacks out of the cart. Tir shook so much he couldn't help noticing. "Are you ill again," he mumbled. "Maybe I'm working you too hard."

Tir straightened her back and looked Bentein straight in the eye. "That man is Norwegian," she said, so angrily she almost spat out the words. "You got three silver marks to bring us across the sea to Ireland. Now you've tricked us. I know you intend for us to be this man's slaves. You've sold us just as the farmers buy cattle at market."

Bentein looked at her in amazement. "How did you get that idea, my girl?" he asked.

Tir was so angry she jumped up and down. "Don't try to trick your way out of it," she almost screamed. Tears spurted from her eyes. "This whole town is full of Norse Vikings."

"Of course it is," said Bentein, calm as a rock. "It's a long time since the Irish ruled over this region. It's said the first people to put up buildings in this town were some Norse Vikings who drove out the inhabitants who lived here before. But as time went on they married Irish girls and grew more peaceful. The Norsemen have settled down all along the coast. They have turned into farmers like us, and are just as afraid of Vikings and other raiders as the Irish themselves. That's how it's been for a hundred years."

Bentein laughed, and then Tir and Reim started to laugh too. The little corner of Ireland they once lived in was so remote that news seldom reached it. Everyone in the tiny village spoke Celtic, and there were no merchants there who sailed backward and forward with foreign wares. When they came to think of it, the monks had talked of a part of Ireland occupied by foreigners. But they'd always somehow imagined that most of what the monks told was a fairy tale. Not until now had they realized how immense the world was.

∼

The next day they walked around the narrow alleyways of Dublin. They turned into a wider street, and suddenly they were on an open square with houses in all directions. It was the town marketplace, teeming with more life and movement than they had ever seen in any other place. The farmers had come in with vegetables and fruit, there were carts filled with turnips and cabbages and shiny red apples, there were eggs and big cheeses, wine in earthenware pitchers, wheat cakes and nuts. Hens fluttered around in cages, oxen bellowed and cows mooed. A flock of sheep had escaped and ran to and fro among the stalls, creating uproar and commotion among the people at the market. They scolded and shook their fists at the poor shepherd trying to get all of his flock together again. He puffed and panted, red as a setting sun in the face as he crawled under the stalls to drag out lambs and big rams. Furious kicks and angry words were showered on him from the market folk. But the townsfolk stood around laughing fit to burst. And some crafty little kids even managed to snatch a lamb or two, giving the poor shepherd even more trouble collecting his flock.

At one end of the market there were stalls for craftsmen selling objects in wood and bone. There were sheaths for long knives, there were pieces made of walrus bone for board games, and there were reliquaries and crosses needed by the priests and monks for churches and monasteries. The wood carver sat outside his booth in the warm sunshine. Many people had gathered around to admire his work. His hands held the knife handle firmly, he bent and twisted the piece of wood to make the strangest intricate patterns. "Did you see that," people nodded, "what a fine craftsman." And as the wood carver was a quick-witted fellow into the bargain and knew how to tell a good story, many people pulled silver from their pockets and exchanged it for a sheath or a spoon with a fine handle.

Then Tir seized Reim's arm. "Look over there," she whispered. Reim turned his head to where she pointed. He jumped. There was a group of people over there tied together with thongs and ropes. They were in the section of the market where oxen and calves were sold. They were bare-chested, and many people walked around examining them. "Fine wares for sale," shouted a powerful red-bearded Viking, "they're all young and fit!" Reim grabbed Tir by the hand and they kept well away from that corner of the market. So that was how it was in Ireland too. The Vikings traveled over to the continent to steal goods and slaves, and as far as they could see there were not only Norsemen stopping to buy. Quite a few wealthy Irishmen were glad of a good working slave, too.

Memories crowded in on Tir. All the misery she and Reim had suffered came back to her when she saw the group of people tied together at the end of the market. She felt powerless. There was nothing she could do. She could only turn away.

"There's Bentein over there," she said suddenly.

Bentein had set himself up with all his sacks of feathers. He had hung the skins up on a kind of stand. He was smiling happily now. It looked as if all the young women in Dublin had gathered around his stall. They caressed the beautiful furs, held them up to their faces and hung them around their necks. And Bentein fooled around winking to them all in turn. Tir and Reim felt a bit safer when they were with Bentein. But they didn't know yet how to get away from Dublin into the country. Their stomachs screamed for food. They looked longingly at the golden loaves some women were selling nearby.

Then something happened.

"Reim," whispered Tir. "Listen carefully!" Among the group of young women they heard a high-pitched voice different from the others. They could hear from the accent she came from their home region. She stood bargaining with Bentein for a fine fur. She was dressed in

a long, red-brown cloak edged with marten fur, with little bells on the sleeves. She had put up her hair in a gold hairnet. She looked most elegant. She and her friend stood turning over the fur, and the woman looked into her leather purse. She laughed. "I'd better ask my husband first. He's hidden away his silver so I won't find it while he's away!"

"I'll be glad to sell the fur for a kiss or two," smiled Bentein, winking at the women. They giggled, took each other by the arm and turned their backs.

At that moment the little leather purse fell to the ground. Reim was there in a flash and picked it up. He bowed before the cloaked woman.

She smiled kindly. She didn't seem to see his ragged clothes and dirty hand. "Thank you, my lad! I haven't much to give you for your kindness, for this purse is as empty as a flour bin after the mice have been there!"

"It doesn't matter," said Reim. "Anyone who hasn't much to begin with doesn't expect more."

The woman's voice grew still kinder. "You must come from the same parts as I do, little rag-bag." She named her home place. It was very close to the village where Reim and Tir had grown up.

"It's a long way from Dublin," she said. "How did you get here? Well, anyway, you certainly look hungry. Come home with me, and I'll give you something."

Fortune smiles on us now, thought Tir to herself as she followed the two women along the narrow alleyways. They passed a lot of little wickerwork booths until they reached a house that was bigger than the others. The women went inside and Reim and Tir followed them. The women set their servant girls to getting some food and wine for the two children, and while they greedily ate up everything on the dish, she sat and chatted with them. Tir and Reim both talked together, and the good wine made them quite dizzy. The woman was horrified when she heard of the long journey they had been on.

Yes, she was well aware the Vikings had ravaged their village. She had seen the smoke drifting over the oak forest, and soon the news reached the place where she lived. Many of the monks had gone there, and many men, women and children who had fled from the burned village. She and her relatives helped as much as they could They nursed the wounded and comforted the terrified children.

Later on she had married a rich Celtic merchant who

lived in Dublin and was friendly with the Norsemen in the town. But she didn't care for the heathen customs kept by some of them, for she herself had been strictly brought up in the Christian faith. She often went out to a small monastery church only half a day's journey away.

Suddenly she had a bright idea. "There's someone at that monastery you may know. Tomorrow I'll show you the way there..."

⌒

To be sure, it was beautiful in Norway, thought Tir. She recalled the fjords where the water was dark green as a dragon's eye, she recalled the dusky blue mountains, the mossy soft forest floor shining with chickweed wintergreen, the deep sighing spruce forests and the rivers gushing angrily and foaming into the fjords.

To be sure, it was beautiful in Iceland, with the rivers like wide silver bands through the pastures, the lava plains with magical rocks and mountains, the birch forest with rustling and singing leaves, and over the mountains the great arms of glaciers shining sparkling white against the blue sky.

But nowhere on earth was so beautiful as Ireland. Nowhere else were the fields so green, nowhere else was the air so high and wide and full of sunlight. Nowhere else did the birds sing so wonderfully.

She sat in the little garden with the monastery buildings around it, and the air seemed to be filled with golden light. A strong scent of spices wafted from the herb garden where thyme and chervil and caraway grew, and big bright yellow and red flowers bloomed. Ivy climbed over the gray walls, with shining dark green leaves. It almost completely hid the monastery. Small birds twittered among the leaves. And how the sun warmed!

"Even if you're not very rich, sister, there's something you have a lot of anyway," said Reim teasingly, "and that's freckles. I can see them popping out while we sit here on the bench. If you get one more you'll look as if you come from Arabia."

"Oh, don't show off," scolded Tir, pulling his red forelock. But her voice was happy. "Just go and lean over the well water over there, you'll soon see we're alike!"

Reim was about to retort, but then gripped her arm: "Hush, he's coming!"

A brown-clad man with a round stomach was coming from the end of the garden. He wore a hood even in the roasting sunshine. They didn't recognize him until he was close up to them. Then he lifted his head and they looked into a pair of good-humored eyes the same color as nuts in autumn.

"Brother Cormac!"

In an instant he reached them and took them into his arms. They stood there for a long, long time under the bright sunshine: they laughed and wept with each other. None of them could get out a word before Brother Cormac raised his head again. "No, now," he said. "The rose just underneath us must have had enough water for a while." He dried his eyes and blew his nose on the sleeve of his cloak.

"Patrick," he said, pinching his ear. "And Sunniva." He tugged her braid and looked at her a long time. "I can't believe it's really you. I must feel you to make sure of it."

Patrick and Sunniva...It was over two years since anyone had called them by those names. They had grown so used to their slave names they had almost forgotten they had been christened in Ireland. Never again would she call her brother Reim. Never again would he shout to his sister and call her Tir. They were called Patrick and Sunniva now.

"Come with me," said Brother Cormac.

He led the way through the little herb garden where the brothers were hoeing the ground. He went through the fruit garden with its old knotted trees that would soon be full of red apples and sweet blue plums. He went into the shadow of the column of pillars, past the small monastery chapel and into a large stone hall.

"Phew," groaned Brother Cormac, drying the sweat from his brow. "We can breathe here, at last." He sat down on the bench.

"We have a lot to tell each other. Such a lot," he said seriously. "But first I want you to have something to eat. You must be hungry."

He had put out some bread and cheese and beakers of wine on the table. "Tuck in, now," he said. "I know how it is for growing foals."

They sat watching every piece the fat monk put in his mouth. They did not take much themselves. But they dared not say anything until Brother Cormac had completely finished. He patted his round stomach and dried his mouth with the back of his hand. Then he looked straight at them and said:

"I know what's on your minds and what you want to ask me about. Just be patient, it will all come out in good time.

You must be wondering how I got here.

When the Vikings attacked our village and burned down the monastery, we brothers decided we must start out on a long journey. Before we left we buried the dead. We took the wounded with us, bound them securely to the horses' backs, and left the village. It was painful to see the smoking heap of ruins behind us. We hadn't been able to save anything from the monastery apart from some leather-bound books some of the brothers took out into the garden as soon as the fire was started. Those books were the only things we had with us when we came to the monastery we live in now. It belongs to the same order of monks as ours. Here we live in peace and quiet as long as it lasts. I ask for nothing more than to be allowed to weed the vegetable garden a bit now and then and read the words of Scripture."

Brother Cormac shook his head. "To think that such a thing could happen to our peaceful little village, no one had expected that..."

But then he brightened up as if woken from his own thoughts. "But now you should see how nice it looks in the village. Every single little house has been rebuilt. The old miller grinds corn as before, the smithy smokes, and the cows and horses graze peacefully out in the pasture. Your father is a clever fellow, Patrick. There isn't a house in the village he hasn't helped to build up from the ground. But then he has a clever wife too. She has enough to do on her own farm, but she always knows where there are people in need of help."

"Hooray for Father! Hooray for Mother!"

"I should say so. It's not more than half a year ago since I saw them last. They're both turned a bit gray since you left them the way you did..."

"And Moira and Cara?"

"Yes, them as well."

"And little brother Roderick?"

"He probably wouldn't like to be called little brother any longer. Last time I saw him he had lost two baby teeth and couldn't whistle very well. He was struggling to manage his new bowstring. The first time, he put the arrow to it the wrong way round, but no one gets to be a brilliant shot in a day."

Patrick and Sunniva laughed. They could imagine their boisterous little brother, who if possible had still more freckles and even brighter red hair than the other siblings.

But Brother Cormac was serious now. A shadow seemed to pass over his good-humored face as if the light faded from the kind brown eyes. "Now comes something I haven't looked forward to telling you. Grandmother

Gaelion is dead!"

The words struck Sunniva like an arrow shot. They cut into her. They hammered and hammered at her heart. Now when everything had turned out so well. Now they were back in their homeland, back to everything known and loved. And now Grandmother Gaelion was dead.

"It was too much for her to see the farmstead burned down and witness the Vikings' plundering. But what was probably worst of all was the two of you being taken prisoner and carried off as slaves. She could never stop thinking about it. I was with her at the end. Before she closed her eyes she said it was as if she could see you there just by her bed. "There they are, my dear children," she said. "Now I know they will come back..."

～

She felt Patrick's hand in hers. It was good to hold as they walked through the little monastery garden. Scents of honey and spices filled the air. The wind played with yellow and white and shining red flowers. Little ants crawled among the stalks. Tiny insects sat on leaves and stems. A butterfly looked like a little yellow flower taking off from the stalk, as it flew and fluttered around in the golden light. It was summertime. It was the season of life. Trees and flowers died each year. But when spring and summer came they woke up as if from a long hibernation to new life. She held on to Patrick's hand tightly, and knew he was thinking the same thing.

Grandmother Gaelion was dead. But she had never felt so strongly that she was still alive all the same. She could see the beloved face among stalks and flowers. She heard her voice in the wind. It whispered of knights and dragons, of trolls and fairies and all the wonderful things that had once upon a time happened in Ireland. The words jingled in her ears, and the pictures she had kept inside her came to life. One day she would make it all known, she thought—all the fine things Grandmother Gaelion had told them. Many would listen and many would wonder over them and remember the dream and the story. And she realized that this was how it was with people one loved. They always lived on in the minds of those who were left behind.

⁓

"Now you must come to the stable with me," said Brother Cormac. "There's something there I want to show you before evening."

They followed him across the pasture where the brothers kept their domestic animals. Some shaggy goats nibbled at tufts of grass and a herd of black and white cows lay dozing close to the warm wall of the monastery. Some tiny gray baby rabbits jumped around in an enclosure.

"Oh dear, there's no peace anywhere any longer," sighed Brother Cormac. "We have to shut the horses in every night because we are afraid of horse thieves. At the monastery here," he pointed across the monastery garden, "we have built a big tower. Every day one of the brothers climbs up in the tower to keep a lookout, so no robbers and warriors attack us. And now we usually keep an axe ready underneath our monk's habit in this part of the country. Whether it's Vikings or countrymen that plunder and rob, it's best to be on guard."

Brother Cormac opened the stable door. It was dim in there, and there was an acrid smell of harness and horse manure. "Wait here," he said, "I'll soon get hold of the mount we shall use when we set out for home."

He went into the darkness of the stable. They heard

him coaxing and chatting to the horses in there. After a few moments he came out with a strong gray mare. She had beautiful shining eyes and a big white star on her forehead.

"Here's a faithful Irish friend I'm sure must remember you," said the monk. "But perhaps you have forgotten her?"

"But it can't be..." said Patrick.

"Can it be?..." said Sunniva. Then her whole face lit up. "But it is! It's Stella!"

Stella! Stella! They both ran to stroke the horse's soft muzzle. The last time they saw her she was a little gray foal jumping around on angular long legs. It was for Stella's sake they had been captured and taken away. When the Vikings came with their dark dragon ships, everyone had fled away into the forest. But when they set fire to the farmhouse, both children had the same thought: Stella is in the stable. Stella will be burned! So they had turned round to let the horse out. That was when they had been captured and carried over the great ocean. "But why is Stella here?"

Brother Cormac stroked the horse's neck. "Your father asked me to take her with me. He didn't feel like keeping her after the farm burned down. But I promised to bring her back one day. I wonder what he'll say when a full-grown mare comes trotting along with two young people he's sure to recognize too."

The monk bent down and pointed at Stella's foot. There was a scar there from a big gash. "When Stella leapt up the slope to get away from the burning farm she tore her foot so badly that for a while we wondered if she would survive. But we looked after her well, and now it seems as if the wound has healed. She limps a bit still, but she trots along all right."

"So we are equal then," said Sunniva. She leaned her head against the horse's flank and kept on stroking the warm soft body. "We both have painful memories of the Vikings, haven't we. I don't think my arm will ever be quite well again."

"D'you think she can carry us both?" asked Patrick.

"I think so," laughed Brother Cormac. "No doubt she'd sink under the weight of a certain glutton of a brother, but she'll probably manage two young sparrows like you."

Sunniva climbed up and Patrick sat behind her. Then they went trotting over the fields and meadows that belonged to the monastery. The mare seemed to understand what a precious load she had on her back. Patrick and Sunniva...Patrick and Sunniva...the hooves sang out. Their slave names were gone forever.

Then it was they discovered the bird. It hovered over them high in the air and went along with them as they rode over the land. Patrick turned his head and pointed:

"Can you see the big bird up there. The one with blue wings. Have you ever seen such an amazing bird before?"

Sunniva smiled. "It has been with us all the time. All the way across the sea to Iceland, and from Iceland back to our green isle. Don't you remember the story Grandmother Gaelion once told us?"

He nodded. Now he understood. A good warm feeling rippled right through him. His eyes were filled with golden light and heavenly blue and summery green.

It was the bird of freedom that hovered up there.